Maggie in the Dark

Transcendence | Book 1

Lynne Cantwell

hearth/myth

Table of Contents

Chapter 1

When I divorced Eugene Brandt and fled from Maryland back to Indiana, leaving behind our three mostly-grown children, I thought I was divorcing his parents, Ruth and Arnie Brandt, too. I needed to leave to save myself – not just from Gene, but from his mother.

So imagine my surprise when I got a call from her nine years later. "Maggie?" she said. "You have to come back."

"What?"

"You have to come back to Rockville. Tomorrow. Next week at the latest."

I laughed at her. "You must be out of your mind, Ruth. Your son was a sick man, and you covered for him. And then when I left him, you turned my children against me. Now I'm supposed to drop everything and rush to your side? Why should I do that?"

"Because…" Her voice broke. "Because Arnie's dead and I've got cancer, and you're the only one I have left."

I guess old habits really do die hard, because two weeks later, I was on the road to suburban Washington, D.C. But I made sure to take my turtle with me.

My own mother loved to tell the story of how I came into possession of the little guy. I was three or four years old, and we were living in the sticks, in a rundown trailer on a county road, while my parents saved up for the house they eventually bought in Lawrenceburg, Indiana. Our lot backed up to the woods, with a farmer's field on the other side. The older kids – my brother Sandy and a couple of his friends – spent a lot of time poking around in the woods, looking for arrowheads and things, and they would take me along if they were in a generous mood.

On this particular day, the boys decided to ditch me. I howled my rage after them, but they didn't come back. So I started kicking at the ground – and something tiddlywinked up and flew a few feet ahead. Startled, I went after it.

It was a copper turtle effigy, a couple of inches long, and shaped like a little bowl with tabs for the turtle legs and head. The top of the shell was pierced in several places and incised with mysterious lines and swirls, and it was grimy as all get-out. But as soon as I held it in my hand, I knew it was mine. Not mine in the "finders keepers" sense; it was more the way you feel when you've misplaced something you love and discover it again somewhere unexpected.

I was not normally a stubborn child, but on this point I dug in my tiny heels and refused to give an inch. That turtle was *mine*, and no one else could touch it. "But Margie," Mom had said, or claimed she'd said, "it's so dirty. Let me clean it up for you."

"No!" I said, and put my hands behind my back.

After a few rounds of this, my mother finally said, "I just don't understand why it's so important to you to hang on to a dirty, ugly thing like that."

"It's not ugly!" I said at last. "It's mine, Mama. It was mine before!"

"Before what?"

"Before!"

I wasn't articulate enough then to explain that I remembered the turtle when it was new. It had been a warm red-brown color, and I'd worn it around my neck on a thong laced through two holes in its shell.

As I got older, I got tired of Sandy trying to swipe the thing to get a rise out of me, so I laced a piece of string through the holes and wore it around my neck. I took pains to keep it out of sight, though; kids will tease you for anything. It wasn't 'til I was in high school that I realized my turtle was more than a thousand years old – an artifact from the Hopewell culture of Mound Builder Indians.

Anyway, Mom told that story over and over, until I was sick of hearing it. Even after she couldn't remember who I was, she would tell her new friend Maggie all about her daughter Margie's turtle. Maybe she'd told it so many times that it had gotten cemented into her brain.

But that was later. She was still doing reasonably well when Ruth summoned me back. Although she was slowing down, as people do as they age, and I was glad to live close enough to run errands for her and take her to her doctor visits.

All right, I know what you're thinking. You think I'm telling you what a good daughter I was so that you'll forget all about the part where I abandoned my children. But Ruth had made those kids more hers than mine.

Look, Gene and I got married pretty young. We met at a party in college, at Indiana University. I was a freshman who wanted to major in anthropology; he was two years ahead of me, a business major, and a handsome fellow – dark hair, dark eyes, olive skin. I have no earthly idea what he saw in me, but all it took was one slow dance to Earth Wind & Fire's "Reasons," and we couldn't get to his room fast enough.

We dated for a year and a half before I got pregnant. I had options – my parents wouldn't have turned me out, and abortion was legal by then – but his mother insisted that we both move in with them. Arnie owned a chain of dry-cleaning stores and gave Gene a management job as a graduation gift, and Ruth helped me plan the wedding – which is to say, she did all the planning and I nodded a lot.

"Now I thought we might book the Willard for the reception," she said. I nodded, although I had no idea what the Willard might be, and I knew she didn't really care what I thought anyway. "And the ceremony will be at the temple, of course."

"Temple?" my mother said when I told her on the phone that night. "Gene is *Jewish*?"

"Well, yeah," I said, "but it's not like he goes to church or anything. Temple, I mean."

"Other than for his own wedding," Mom said dryly. "Why don't you suggest a nice, non-denominational location instead?"

"Absolutely not," said Ruth, horrified. "Why would you even *suggest* it? Why, for a nice Jewish girl like you…to…" She stopped and peered closely at me. "Oh, my God. You're not, are you?" She sat back abruptly and fanned herself with one hand. "Oh, my God!"

The Willard became the venue for both the ceremony and the reception. But it was hardly the last time Ruth and I tussled over religion. I had to put my foot down when she tried to convince us to send the kids to a Jewish day school. Why she pushed it, I never knew; public school had been good enough for Gene and his sisters. But Ruth took our kids to temple with her, and all three of them have Hebrew middle names.

As I said, the kids are grown up now. Beatrice is my eldest. She's a psychologist in Baltimore, and married to a doctor of internal medicine named John Simms – which I learned from my other children; Bea stopped speaking to me when I moved out. Emily, my middle daughter, is finishing graduate school on the West Coast. And my youngest, Tim, is…well. Tim is Tim.

I'll never forget the last night we were all together as a family – and not in a good way. The family would literally fly apart the next day: Emmy was leaving in the afternoon from BWI for freshman orientation at Pepperdine, which started the following day. The shipping company was coming by in the morning to pick up her things, which were mostly already packed in boxes – Em was mailing them to her aunt Abby, who lived near Malibu and who had volunteered to help her move into her dorm. Bea was leaving the day after; she would drive herself to Baltimore to begin her senior year at Johns Hopkins. And I was leaving for Indiana. I'd spent the summer there, helping Mom deal with things after my father died suddenly of a stroke, and I already had a job and an apartment waiting.

Gene and I called a family meeting. "So you guys know your father and I are splitting up," I began.

"News flash," said Tim dismissively.

"Do we have to do this?" asked Bea.

I ignored her. "I want you all to know that none of this is your fault."

"We *know*, Mom," said Bea. "We're not four years old. Can I go? I have things to do."

"No, you may not," said Gene. "Be quiet, Beatrice. This is important."

I tried not to stare at him. It wasn't often that he backed me up. "Uh, well…I just wanted you all to know that even though I won't be living here in this house anymore, I still love you, and I'll always be your mom. And you'll always have a place with me. A home. No matter what."

"What happens to the house?" Bea asked.

Gene and I both stared at her. "What?" Gene asked.

"I mean, most of the time when parents split up, the mom keeps the house and the kids stay with her," Bea said. "But Mom's not staying. So what happens to the house?"

Gene and I traded a look. "We haven't talked about it yet," I said.

"You'll barely be here anyway," Gene said.

"I know, but…" She huffed a breath. "I was just asking, that's all."

"Well, we'll tell you when we figure it out," said Gene. "Anyone else? Emily? Tim?"

Tim glanced at me and away. "I want to stay with Dad."

I'd thought he would, but it still felt like a punch in the gut to hear him say it. But I rallied and said, "That's fair. I wouldn't ask you to move in your senior year if there was any way around it, and there is."

He nodded without looking at me again.

"Em?" I prodded. "You've been really quiet."

"Not much to say," she said with a shrug. "It's not a big deal for me. I was going to stay with Aunt Abby for most of my school breaks anyway. And I think we all knew it was coming."

Bea let out a breath. "Yeah. It's kind of a relief, to be honest. It's been a lot calmer around here this summer with you gone."

"Damn, Bea," Tim said. "Twist the knife a little harder, why don't you?"

"Language, Tim," Gene said. He said nothing at all to Bea.

Em looked at me, alarmed. "She didn't mean it the way it sounded, Mom."

"Yes, she did," I said, more calmly than I felt. I realized that Ruth still had the power to hurt me. She had poisoned my relationship with my children, and I hadn't been there to stop her.

The first time Ruth called me to come back, I told her no, flat out. But she kept calling and pleading with me, and it got so I started to feel sorry for her. Arnie had died the year before – he'd just dropped dead at his desk, she said. Debbie, Gene's eldest sister, was dead to her; she had her own life in New Orleans and refused to come home to help. Debbie's kids were no good – their mother had poisoned them against their grandmother. (That sounded familiar, but I kept my mouth shut.) The middle kid, Abby, had just landed a part in a big movie and couldn't get away. Gene had remarried – a fact that my kids had kept from me – and his new wife was a shrew.

He married his mom, did he? I set that uncharitable thought aside and kept listening.

That left my kids. But Tim was gallivanting around the globe, Bea couldn't get the time off work, and Emmy wasn't speaking to her. "There is literally no one else, Maggie," she said. "You *have* to come."

"What makes you think *I* can take time off work? The Family and Medical Leave Act won't apply – we're not related anymore."

"Oh, just tell them at your little job that you need a vacation."

That made me angry. My *little job* wasn't as little as she thought. I'd been working for our local riverboat casino since the divorce was final. I was trained as a dealer to start with, and this would-be anthropologist was fascinated by the behavior of our guests and their belief in Lady Luck. The Lady had certainly helped *me*; I'd just recently been promoted off the floor and into the back office.

"I've already used up all my vacation time for the year," I said. It was true. What little I got, I'd spent taking Mom back and forth to the doctor. She was a few years older than Ruth, and had quit driving a couple of years before.

"Call in sick, then," she said. "You have to help me, Maggie. There's no one else!"

I sighed. "Let me think about it."

Once I was off the phone with her, I called Emmy. No, she hadn't seen the email from Nana. Nana, she said, was in the habit of sending her chain emails, stupid jokes, and heaps of unsolicited advice. "I finally just got tired of it and blocked her," she said. "Anything I get from her goes right into my spam folder now."

"Well, she says she's got cancer."

"Wait," she said. "She called you?"

"I did mention that, didn't I?"

"Well, yeah, but...*she* called *you?*"

"Believe me," I said. "I was as surprised as you are. Did you know Papa died?"

"Yeah," she said. "Bea told me he killed himself."

I was silent for a moment. "Nana said he dropped dead at his desk."

"More or less," she said. "Blew his brains out. Something about the feds being after him for money laundering." She snickered. "Imagine that. A dry cleaner laundering money."

"That's hilarious," I said absently, mentally reviewing the rest of what Ruth had said. "What's this about Aunt Abby getting a fabulous part in some movie?"

"Oh, jeez," Emmy said with a sigh. "Leave it to Nana to be dramatic. It's not a movie – it's a TV commercial, and she's already done shooting it."

"So she could go," I said.

"No, Mom. She has a day job."

"So do I!"

"We all do. And nobody wants to bend over backwards for Nana because she's been so awful to all of us. She's gonna have to hire someone."

But if the feds are investigating the business, she may not have the money. I left that unsaid, though. Instead I asked, "What's this about your father remarrying?"

"Oh. Yeah." Silence.

"Emily?"

She sighed again. "I told Tim we should have told you." She was quiet for a moment. "Remember Riley?"

Oh, boy. Did I ever remember Riley.

It had been a lovely summer evening – warm, but not nearly as sticky as usual. Gene had been working late a lot, and I was going stir-crazy at home with the kids all day. Bea was in middle school by then, but Em and Tim were still in grade school, and all three of them were at that age where they would take offense if a sibling so much as looked at them cockeyed.

"Let's surprise Dad!" I said that night.

"Like, you mean, go to the shop?" Emmy asked, sitting up straight. "Can we go for ice cream after?"

"I'll stay here," said Bea in her best bored tone.

"You will not," I said. "We're all going. Tim, put your game down."

"Can't I take it with?"

"No."

"Aw, Mom." But he tossed the device on the coffee table and rummaged under the sofa for his beat-up Chucks.

"He won't be there," Bea said as I herded the kids out to the car.

I opened the door and stared at her. "What do you mean? Of course he'll be there. Where else would he be?"

She looked uncomfortable, but she didn't say anything else. She just got in the car.

Bea was half right. Gene was in his office, but he wasn't working. However, Riley, his newest high school intern, was working very hard indeed. Luckily, I went in first. "Look who's here!" I announced grandly as I swung open his office door. Then, taking in the scene, I body-blocked the opening and shut the door as fast as I could.

"Why can't we go in?" Tim asked.

"Daddy's wrapping something up," I said, realizing what I'd said only after the words were out of my mouth. Thank God the kids were too young to get the double entendre. At least, I hoped they were too young.

"What's he doing?" asked Bea, suddenly very interested.

"Can we still get ice cream?" asked Emmy.

The door swung open. Gene had zipped up his pants and plastered a big smile on his face. "Hey, everybody! Good job! You really surprised me!" He hugged all the kids and gave me a peck on the cheek.

"We all missed you so much," I said, itching to rake my fingernails across that jovial face.

"Next time, call ahead, maybe," he said.

The fight we had that night was epic, despite being conducted entirely in whispers so as not to wake the kids. In the end, Gene apologized for hurting me. He promised to stop seeing Riley, and he promised to go to marriage counseling.

He never did either one. And I began to realize that Riley wasn't the first. Nor was she the last. And yes, Bea had known; one of her classmates was Riley's younger sister. I'd been chalking up Bea's attitude to middle school truculence, but in fact she was disgusted with both of us: her father for his behavior, and me for not seeing what was going on, right under my nose.

I demanded that he cancel the internship program, or at least stop using it as a recruiting tool for his dalliances – but I might as well have been trying to corral a hurricane for all the good it did. Gene had won Civic Leader of the Year for the internship program. He refused to do anything that would jeopardize his image in the community.

"What if word gets around?" I hissed that first night. "People talk, you know. Where will your precious image be then?"

Without another word, he turned over and flipped off the light.

I can't remember whether it was the third or fourth time we had that same fight, but it dawned on me that he was never going to change. Why should he? He had everything he wanted: a nice house, a lovely wife and three lovely children, a thriving business, and a little something on the side.

I realized Emily was still talking. "I guess she ran into him, or he ran into her, or something," she said. "Anyway, they started seeing each other again."

"When was this?"

"Not long after the divorce was final."

My eyes widened. "He didn't waste any time, did he?" I blurted. Then, "I'm sorry. I shouldn't have said that." He was her father, after all.

"Don't be sorry," Em said. "We all thought the same thing." The wedding, she said, was a couple of years later.

We said goodbye shortly after that, and I hung up. Then I picked up one of the throw pillows beside me on the couch and hugged it against my midsection – as if I'd been split open and was trying desperately to keep my insides from falling out.

We had been divorced for eight years. His new marriage was old news. And still it felt like I'd been kicked in the stomach.

I'd been out on a date or two since the divorce, but I hadn't found anybody I liked well enough to make it a regular thing. I told myself I enjoyed being single and unencumbered, but that was only part of the truth. The rest of it was that even now, Ruth controlled me. I didn't date because I didn't want to risk having someone like her in my life again.

Well, so much for that worry. Ruth *herself* was back. In fact, she'd never left. And after my chat with Emmy, my interest in Ruth's crazy plan was piqued in a way my ex-mother-in-law could not have engineered – because now I wanted to find out what else she had lied about.

Chapter 2

In the end, the turtle made the decision for me.

I'd made a special spot for it in my bedroom. It was centered on an end table, flanked by a fat candle that I lit now and then, and a small, shallow basket I'd picked up at a crafts fair. Sometimes I'd put rocks or feathers in the basket – whatever I found on my walks around the neighborhood.

Anyway, I pulled the gold chain over my head, lit the candle, and sat for a few moments with my eyes closed, centering myself. Then I thought about Ruth's demand, and the trip I would have to take to get there, and what it would mean to dredge up all that stuff I'd thought long buried. I was just beginning to frame an actual question when a voice sounded in my head:

GO.

My eyes flew open. In all the years I had had my turtle, and all the times I had come to it worried or confused or afraid, I had never received a verbal response before. Feelings or vibrations, yes. But words? Commands? Because there was nothing even remotely like a suggestion in that one-word message. Whether it was the turtle or the god it represented, I'd clearly been given the order to march.

So I called my mom and told her I'd be going out of town for a couple of weeks. "This is all fairly sudden," Mom said, her voice quavering a bit. "Where are you going?"

"An old…acquaintance needs me," I said.

"It's Ruth," Mom said in disgust. "It's gotta be. Nobody else would feel so *entitled*."

I could tell she was also scared. If I were in Maryland, I wouldn't be around to help her out.

"It is," I confirmed. There didn't seem to be a reason to lie to her. "But it'll be okay, Mom. We'll do a big grocery store run right before I leave. And I'll call Sandy. It's about time he and Diane pitched in more, anyway." My brother and his wife lived in Indianapolis, about an hour and a half away.

Mom grumbled, but it was mostly for show. She knew I was going to go.

So there I was, on that day in late October of 2015, on the interstate east of Columbus, Ohio. As I passed through the Buckeye Lake region, a brown highway sign caught my eye: *Great Circle Earthworks*, it said. The "Great Circle" part sounded like New Age mumbo-jumbo. Or maybe it was a haven for refugees from the 1960s. Didn't the hippies make earthworks out of old pop bottles and dirt? Or maybe those were earthships. It didn't appear to matter, for the car was already on the exit ramp, although I didn't remember turning the wheel.

A few miles north, I found myself in small-town America: car dealerships, fast-food joints, and strip shopping centers. And then I saw the sign across the divided highway on the left: *Newark Earthworks*. I made an awkward U-turn at the next light and found myself in a tiny parking lot, a decrepit VW bus the only other vehicle parked there. It seemed my guess about hippies might have been right, after all.

It was a beautiful fall afternoon, if a little chilly. The sky was cloudless and the trees around the site were changing color in spectacular fashion. I'd been on the road for a couple of hours already. I thought a little leg-stretcher around the park would do me good.

I got out of the car and began to walk up the asphalt path. A tall earthen berm, its top higher than my head, ran parallel to the path on my left. As I walked, my upper chest felt itchy; I touched the turtle and realized it was vibrating. No, buzzing. It was definitely buzzing.

The earthen berm ended at the opening to a meadow; a second berm, the same height as the first, began a short distance away. I stepped toward the opening and realized what I was seeing was a single berm that circled the tree-dotted meadow. A deep ditch also circled the meadow's edge inside the berm.

I stepped inside the gate – for a gate it had to be – and fell to my knees, clutching my middle in sudden pain and fighting an urge to howl. All the grief I'd stuffed down for all these years so I could function in the world – my father's death, Gene's betrayal, Ruth's meddling, Bea's rejection, Tim's decision to stay with his father – even the loss of the career I'd hoped for – hit me all at once, and at full force, as if I were experiencing them all for the first time.

I don't know how long I knelt there as tears ran down my face. At last, still pretty out of it, I got to my feet and wandered among the trees, heedless of direction. I found myself walking up a smaller mound in the center of the meadow. My turtle was vibrating so hard I could hear it humming, and all at once I knew why: This was where I had received it, in that other life so long ago. I blinked, and saw a wooden palisade where the mound's wings stood in my time. The scent of smoke was in the air – not tobacco smoke, and not the smell of burning leaves, but an odor of scorched herbs with an underlying stench of rot. A man wearing a copper breastplate and copper antlers was saying something to me in a language I could almost understand. Then he held out the turtle, warm and untarnished, the meaning of every line on its shell known to me. I allowed the shaman to lay it upon my outstretched palms. He laced the thin thong – not leather, I saw now, but sinew – through the holes in the turtle's back, and tied the ends in a strong knot. When he placed the string around my neck, the crowd behind me roared. I turned to acknowledge the approval of my people…

And I faced the empty meadow with my arms raised in benediction, the crowd's yips and howls fading fast on the sudden breeze. That loss, too, crowded in around me, and I wept again.

At last, I stumbled back out the way I had come in.

I had no idea what I'd just experienced. Was it a past life regression? If so, was it triggered by the turtle effigy or by my emotional reaction upon entering the circle? And if it was the latter, why did I have to go through all that grief first?

In search of answers, I meandered toward the visitors' center, where a bronze plaque explained the site's significance:

HERE THE HOPEWELL INDIANS, WHO BUILT THE COMPLEX SOME TWO THOUSAND YEARS AGO, PARTICIPATED IN SOCIAL AND RELIGIOUS OBSERVANCES.

That confirmed my experience to some extent. But I still had no frame of reference for it. Nothing like it had ever happened to me before.

I looked over the rest of the plaque, which included a map of the site. I studied that map for quite some time, hoping some feature on it would trigger another rush of memory. Maybe if I could walk the old roads...

I walked around the visitors' center to find a path to the square I'd seen on the map, and realized it was gone. The intersection where I'd made the U-turn was right where the path should have been, and across the road was more small-town America.

Deflated, I retraced my steps to the visitors' center and began the walk back to the car.

"Margie!" someone called from the Great Circle's entrance. "There you are!"

I looked toward the speaker – the only other person I'd seen since my arrival. She was elderly, but by no means frail; she walked very fast, with a spring in her step. She wore a powder-blue tracksuit and sensible white walking shoes, much scuffed. Her eyes, I noticed as she approached, were a clear, startling blue behind her glasses, and her cheeks glowed in the chilly air. "Margie!" she called again, with a smile.

"Ma'am, were you talking to me? My name's Maggie," I said. My given name is Margaret May, and I'd been called Margie all through school. But when I heard Rod Stewart singing about Maggie May, I decided I liked Maggie better – never mind that the song was about an older woman who led a teenage boy astray. The point is that I'd been Maggie for probably thirty years by then, although my mother still slipped up occasionally. Maybe this woman was a friend of Mom's?

"Sorry," she said. "Of course it's Maggie. Here, child, come with me." She slipped past me on the asphalt path and took off down the hill toward the parking lot, her gray braid bouncing on her back.

"Ma'am? I really need to be going," I called after her.

"This won't take long," she shouted over her shoulder without breaking her stride.

Well, I had to go that way anyway to get back to my car. And maybe this odd woman knew something about the Great Circle that would help me figure out what had happened to me in there. So I followed her.

She walked right to the VW bus and knocked on the side. The door slid open and a grizzled fellow popped out. "Hey, Granny. Did you find her?" he asked. Granny hooked a thumb toward me and said something I was too far away to hear. The man looked toward me and called, "Oh, hey! Good to meet you. Come on in." He scooted aside to let Granny hop in while beckoning to me with one hand. Seeing my hesitation, he gave me a crooked grin. "It's okay. We don't bite, I promise."

"I really do have to get back on the road," I said, hauling myself into the van.

Still grinning, he stuck out a hand. "Zedediah Jones. Pleased to meet you."

"Maggie Muir," I said, and shook. Muir was my maiden name. I was still a Brandt legally, but I wasn't comfortable about giving these folks my real name.

Up close, I could see that Zedediah Jones wasn't nearly as old as I'd thought. His long hair was tied back in a neat ponytail, and his gray mustache was bushy but trimmed. He wore a tie-dyed t-shirt and faded jeans, of course, under his navy blue peacoat.

He gave Granny a surprised look. "Why'd you call her Margie?"

"I forgot." The old woman waved a hand dismissively as she eased onto the bench seat. "Here, child. Sit next to me."

"What's funny," I said as I sat, "is that I used to go by Margie. Were you a friend of my parents?"

"No."

"Did you ever live in…?"

"No. This isn't about that. Hold out your hand."

I glanced at Zedediah in surprise. He nodded. "Go on. It's safe."

I don't know why I was turning to him as the arbiter of what was safe, but when he said that, I did as she had asked. She grabbed it and studied my palm. "You found the turtle. Good."

My left hand reflexively grabbed for the turtle under my shirt. She saw the movement and her eyes widened a bit. "You wore it inside the Great Circle? That must have been quite an experience."

I swallowed. "It was. Can you tell me what it was about? The ceremony when I got the turtle, I mean."

She sighed and dropped my hand. "Probably not. That was all before my time."

At first I thought she was joking – two thousand years ago was *before my time* for all of us – but the only person smiling was me.

"What I have to tell you is only tangentially related to the people who built this site." She must have noticed my shoulders slump, because she quickly added, "But it has a direct bearing on why you're here on this planet at this time in its history."

Why you're here on this planet… That seemed a little New-Agey to me. "Okay, then. Suppose you tell me why you think I'm here."

She leaned back in her seat. "All right. What do you know about this site?"

"Nothing." I shook my head. "Less than nothing. I've driven this stretch of I-70 many times, but I've never seen that sign before. All I know is that the Hopewell Indians built it."

"You read that on that plaque," she said, and I nodded. "The Hopewell were a Native American tribe or culture that lived around the time of the birth of Christ. They built this site sometime between 100 and 500 A.D., by hand. They made the berms by carrying dirt in hand-woven baskets, one basketful at a time. They dug the ditches with tools made of bone, and lined them with clay so they would hold water."

I tried to recall whether I'd seen water in those ditches during my vision, but concluded there were too many people in the way. "Why?" I asked. "What were the berms and ditches for?"

"Nobody knows for sure. A lot of mound-building cultures used earthworks as tombs, but archaeologists haven't found any graves here. There were some in an elliptical earthwork a few miles from here, but that site is gone now. A lot of ancient earthworks have been destroyed over the years."

I nodded again, thinking of the intersection that had been plopped in the midst of the avenue leading to the square. I figured the modern road builders weren't the first to dig up that older road.

"But today, we know at least part of the reason that the ancients built this site," she went on. "Astronomers have been out here to see whether the Hopewell incorporated sightlines in their structures for events in the sky."

"Like Stonehenge?" I said. "And...what's the one in Ireland? Newgrange."

"Exactly like those. And in fact, the Hopewell had built those into their earthworks." She leaned forward and pointed out the windshield. "You can't see it from here, but a few miles away is another big Hopewell earthwork. Two of them, in fact – a circle, smaller than the Great Circle but with a diameter of one-thousand-fifty-four feet, and an eight-sided figure called the Octagon. Astronomers have discovered that the walls of the Octagon were constructed to align with certain positions of the moon."

"Like moonrise and moonset?"

"Yes, but it's more complicated than that." She sat back. "You know that the moon circles the earth in 28 days, more or less. We can track its cycle easily enough by watching its phases. And at the extreme ends of the cycle, the movement seems to slow – so that it looks to us like the moon is full for three days each month, and dark for another three days.

"The spot on the horizon where the moon rises and sets changes, too, and those points oscillate from maximum to minimum on an 18.6-year cycle. And just like with the monthly cycle, there's a period at the extremes when the moonrise and moonset points don't appear to change much at all – except instead of lasting three days, the major and minor lunar standstills last three years each. And the Hopewell built those points – for the major and minor lunar standstills – into their design for the Octagon. That means they could predict when major and minor standstills would happen."

"Why?" I asked.

"We don't know for sure," Granny said. "But it may be no accident that they designed those readings into a major ceremonial site. We believe they had devised a cycle of ceremonies that would renew the earth, and the readings they took at the Octagon told them when those ceremonies should be held." She pointed at the spot where my turtle hung under my shirt. "Have you heard the phrase Turtle Island?"

I shook my head.

"Many Woodland Indian tribes have a creation myth that states North America is the shell of a giant turtle. For them, we all live on Turtle Island."

I started. "The markings on my turtle…" I shook my head. "What you said just now jogged something loose. In my vision inside the circle, I understood the markings. The memory is gone again. But it had something to do with this earth renewal you're talking about." I shook my head again. "Crazy."

"Not crazy," she said. "Not crazy at all. Look, Margie…"

"Maggie," I said automatically.

She waved her hand impatiently. "It doesn't matter. It's not your real name anyway."

I was so surprised at that that I nearly missed the rest of what she had to say.

"What I'm trying to get at is that we're now at the point of a minor lunar standstill. It's occurring this month. Things are going to start happening again very soon."

"What do you mean by that?"

"Have you felt like life has been on hold for you?"

I shrugged. "Not particularly. Wait. Maybe." I *had* been running in place for the past few years. I had a good job at the casino, but there was no further advancement there. My relationship with my kids hadn't gotten worse, but it hadn't gotten any better, either. And my love life had been D.O.A. for years. "But things are changing now," I said. "I'm on my way to Maryland to help a sick…friend." Close enough, I thought. "And while I was preparing for the trip, I learned a lot of things have been happening that I didn't know about."

"Yes," she said, nodding emphatically. "We're coming out of the bottom of the cycle. Things are going to begin to change. But first, some things have to end."

I frowned. "What does *that* mean?"

She took both of my hands and closed her eyes. "Three doors will close to you," she intoned in a deeper voice than she had used up to now, "and you will close three more of your own free will. Then, and only then, will the right door open. When that occurs, you must walk through, and quickly, because it will not stay open long. Attend! For it is only by humanity's renewal that the Earth itself may be renewed. Kokumthena Herself charges you with this task. Do not fail!"

Her last three words seemed to reverberate in a much bigger space, and with them came a wild wind redolent with the scent of freshly turned dirt and clean, life-giving rain.

She dropped my hands and slumped against the cushions. In a moment, she began to snore.

"Come on," Zedediah said. "She needs to sleep it off." He slid the door open and helped me out.

I looked at him appraisingly. "What was all that about, anyway?"

He scratched at his neck. "It's a little hard to explain."

"I bet," I said. "All right, then. Who's Kokumthena?"

"That one, I can answer. She's the creator goddess of the Shawnee Indians." He looked around. "They lived here in the Scioto River valley after the Adena and the Hopewell had moved on. They kind of took over responsibility for these sacred sites, in a way, although I guess they never understood what they were built for. Or maybe they lost that knowledge the same way they lost so much of their own history and spirituality, after the U.S. government marched them off to Oklahoma."

"Are you Shawnee?" I asked quietly.

"Nah," he said with a laugh. "It's just that hanging around with Granny kind of rubs off on you after a while."

"Is *she* Shawnee?"

"I'm not sure," he said, "but she thinks she's Kokumthena."

My eyes widened. "Does she have dementia?"

"Is she delusional, do you mean?" He leaned his back against the side of the bus and shoved his hands in his coat pockets. "Maybe. Maybe not. She knew she was going to find you here today. I drove all night from Wisconsin to get us here." He patted the side of the van. "This here's *my* bus. I've had it since '69. Bought it off a guy who drove it to Woodstock. Still runs like a dream – well, with a little help now and then." He grinned at me.

"So are you and Granny related?"

"Are we married, is what you want to know." He grinned again. "Nope, and we're not having sex, either, because that will be your next question. I'm just helping her out."

"Helping her?"

"She needs to find her one-thousand-fifty-four people," he said. "The magical Hopewell unit of measurement. You're number 550, by the way. We're a little ahead of schedule, but she's worried she may slow down toward the end."

"The end of what?" This was getting more confusing by the minute.

"The cycle," he said. "The lunar cycle." He must have seen that I was still puzzled, because he said, "She has about nine-and-a-half years to find the rest of you, and then *she'll* be renewed. We all have our own role to play in renewing the earth, see. Mine's to drive the bus." He slapped the side of the van again, then glanced through the window. "Speaking of which, we'd all better get moving. You've still got a long drive ahead of you, and so do we. We're headed to Cahokia next. Granny says the Cahokians weren't her people, but she needs to see somebody over there and that's the most convenient spot for the meetup."

"Well, safe travels, Zedediah," I said, and held out my hand.

He shook it. "You can call me Zed. And you're Maggie. I'll make sure she doesn't forget again."

"Thanks." I extracted my hand and began walking toward my car. "Nice to meet you, Zed."

"See you later, Maggie," he called. I waved at him over my shoulder, and tried to believe his last words were a standard-issue parting, and not a promise – or a threat.

Chapter 3

I had a lot to think about as I drove the rest of the way to Maryland. Who *was* Granny, anyway? Was she crazy? Did she have some kind of past-life regression thing going on, the way I might have had in the Great Circle? Or was she who she said she was – the Shawnee creator goddess, reincarnated?

Maybe not reincarnated, exactly. Did the Shawnee even believe in reincarnation?

And what was it she'd said about my future? Three doors would close for me, and I would close three more. And then a door would open. No, then the *right* door would open.

I wondered whether this so-called right door had anything to do with the vision or hallucination or whatever-it-was that I'd experienced in the Great Circle. But if so, it had opened too soon. So maybe the vision had shut a door? And if so, which one?

Maybe it had shut the door on my sanity. Maybe I'd end up as crazy as Granny before this was all over. I was feeling a little unhinged already. Why else had I let Ruth, of all people, talk me into driving all this way to help her?

Maybe I would show up at Ruth's house, only to have her slam the door in my face. But that seemed too literal an interpretation of Granny's words. And anyway, I thought I'd closed the door on this part of my life before, when I moved back to Indiana. But maybe I'd left something undone. Maybe Bea…

No. Beatrice herself had closed that door. If our relationship were to have a happy ending, I'd have to twist Granny's prophecy into contortions to get it to fit.

But I owed it to myself, and to my eldest daughter, to try. And I wanted to meet my grandchildren, darn it. It was time I reclaimed my family from Ruth.

Do you have any idea how hard it is for a mother to decide to leave her children? Because I knew I would have to. Ruth would have never let my kids out of her clutches. She had assigned them roles, much as she had with her own children, and she expected them to live up to them.

Poor Bea took the brunt of it. Ruth was convinced she was academically gifted and pushed her to take every advanced class offered by her high school. The workload stressed her out, but she gritted her teeth and hung on. Once – only once – I gave her permission to ease up. "I don't like what this stress is doing to you," I told her one morning at breakfast. That is, I was having breakfast; she was gulping coffee as she frantically tried to finish a math assignment. "What time did you go to bed?"

"I didn't," she said. "I fell asleep at my desk while I was trying to get this done."

"See? That's what I mean. Come on, Bea, put that aside and eat." When she ignored me, I said, "You don't have to be the family brainiac, you know."

At last, she looked at me. "Of course I do. I can't disappoint Nana."

"She's not the last word in your life!" I said.

"Mom!" she yelled. "Can we *not* have this discussion now? I have to turn this in in forty-five minutes!"

I left her alone then. I didn't want anyone to accuse me of jeopardizing her academic success. But I mentioned the conversation to Bea's therapist. I don't know whether anything ever came of it, though – Bea's behavior never changed.

Ruth assigned Tim the role of family athlete and made sure he tried out for a sport every season. He was never a star, but he did pretty well. He even made it onto a travel team for soccer, with my full support. Not because I had dreams of my son winning a soccer scholarship someday –

I'd seen him play – but because his father always took him to the tournaments, and those weekend trips pulled Gene away from his latest little girl.

Emmy dreamed her way through school. I privately thought she was smarter than her older sister, but Em didn't have the same drive to excel that Bea had; her grades were only average. Ruth didn't know what to do with her, much as she hadn't known what to do with Abby, who had stayed in California after she finished college and was picking up acting gigs here and there. On that basis, I think, Ruth decided Em must be the artistic type and tried to push her into the arts – theater or music. Ceramics. Photography. Something. Anything! But Em, bless her, refused to be pushed. She took enrichment classes to make her grandmother happy, but I knew her heart wasn't in any of them.

My suspicions about Emmy's giftedness were confirmed when we got her SAT results. She'd racked up a perfect score – something her "brainiac" older sister hadn't come close to achieving. "You know every college in America will be recruiting you, right?" I said.

She sighed. "Yeah, I know." She tossed the paper with her scores aside.

"But you should be proud of yourself!" I said. "The whole world is open to you. What do you want to do with your life?"

She answered as if she hadn't been listening. "Do we have to tell Nana what I got?"

"What?"

"Can we, like, lie? Can we tell her my scores sucked?"

My heart went out to her, but I had to be honest. "That won't work forever. At some point, she's going to figure it out. Probably when she reads in the paper that the National Merit Scholarship people have given you some major prize or other."

She scowled. "Yeah."

"Emily," I said, leaning toward her, "listen to me. Pick a college far away from her. She can't run your life forever."

She snorted. "Sure, she can. She's been running *your* life ever since you married Dad."

I held her gaze. "Well," I said. "You're not wrong."

It was still true. But I resolved to undo at least some of the damage Ruth had caused me and mine.

Occupied by my thoughts as I was, the trip seemed to whiz by. But night had fallen, and as I rounded the last corner to my former in-laws' house, time seemed to slow. Or maybe I just eased off the gas pedal, reluctant to get where I was going.

For all of Ruth and Arnie's efforts to rub elbows with the best people in D.C., their house was nothing special: a rambling split-level in a regular subdivision – no nicer, really, than my own parents' house, although I suspected Mom and Dad's house in small-town Indiana had cost about a tenth of what the Brandts had paid for this place. *Location, location, location*, as the real estate folks say.

I remembered suddenly that Gene had liked to take drives through Potomac and Chevy Chase, just to drool over the expensive real estate. He dreamed of buying a house there, and he used to ask his parents how come they'd never moved.

"What's wrong with this house?" Arnie would say. "It fits us just fine, it's close to my office, and it's paid for. Why go into debt just to live in one of those snobby neighborhoods?"

Sometimes I'd cut a glance at Ruth during these conversations, and I'd catch a sour look on her face – as if she'd had the same argument with Arnie and for once, he had won.

I navigated the city streets with a sinking feeling, remembering again how much I'd hated it here. Sometimes, it had seemed to me, between the multi-lane streets and the shopping center parking lots, the whole town was paved over. Summers were hot and sticky and lasted forever. And the people were less friendly than at home. I'd missed small-town life and knowing my neighbors. I'd missed being able to sit outside in the summer without feeling like the air was smothering me.

But it's not summer now. And it's only for a couple of weeks this time. You can stand it again for that long. I sighed, straightened my shoulders, and tried to look happier about being back.

Ruth's driveway, lined with solar lights on stakes, was empty of cars, the garage door shut tight. The porch light was off, though Ruth knew I was coming. The house, too, looked dark, although the blue light of a television wavered in the living room and a fluorescent bulb flickered in the kitchen. I knew exactly where that fluorescent fixture hung above the sink, and muscle memory was telling me, even now, how many steps there were between the sink and the stove, the stove and the fridge.

You're stalling. Just get on with it. I sighed again and got out of the car.

The street lights lit the yard well enough that I made it to the front door without a mishap. I had long since thrown away my key to this house, so I rang the doorbell and waited.

And waited.

I was on the verge of ringing the bell again when I heard someone shuffling to the door. "Hang on," Ruth muttered, loudly enough that I could hear her. Then the porch light came on, blinding me briefly, and the door opened. "Why didn't you just come in?" she demanded.

As a young bride, that peremptory tone had made me want to apologize, even when there had been nothing for me to apologize for. Now, it just irritated me. "Because I don't live here anymore," I replied tartly. "Hello to you, too."

She had shrunk – or maybe she just loomed larger in my memory. I was taller than her now by a good couple of inches. Her hair, which had always been professionally dyed and styled, was white and wispy, and her slight figure seemed swallowed up by a plush white bathrobe.

She gave me the same once-over that I had given her, and finally said, "Well, come in, then." She motioned me away from the door and began to shut it, then paused. "Don't you have a suitcase or something?"

"I'll go out and get it in a little while," I said. "Let's chat first." To be honest, I still wasn't sure I was going to stay, and I didn't want to have to wrestle my stuff inside, only to turn around and wrestle it back out to the car again.

"Suit yourself," she said, and pushed the door shut. "Come on in here." She headed toward the living room – and now I saw why she was shuffling: she was wearing a pair of outsized slippers.

"Where did you get those?" I asked, pointing at her feet.

"They were Arnie's. Mine wore out." She eased herself into a recliner with a *whoof*. Clearly she spent a lot of time there – the TV remote, a water glass, a box of tissues, and other odds and ends sat on low tables that flanked the chair. She turned on the lamp next to the chair and muted the TV. "So. You can stay in Debbie's room. That will be convenient, as it's right next to mine – in case I need help in the middle of the night."

My eyes widened. "Help with what?"

"Well, *I* don't know. I've never had cancer before," she said.

It dawned on me that at least part of her snappishness stemmed from fear. I sat forward and rested my forearms on my knees. "What kind of cancer do you have? And what's the prognosis?"

She pulled her robe tighter. "Where did you pick up all that medical jargon, anyway?"

"TV shows," I said, and waited.

She glared at me as if I'd offended her – another look I remembered from years past – but finally responded. "Uterine cancer. I have to have my ovaries cut out." She frowned in distaste. "And then I have to go for radiation."

"I think they'll take out more than your ovaries, Ruth," I said.

She waved a hand in dismissal. "All I heard was they were gonna cut me open."

"That's pretty scary."

She grunted and looked at the TV.

"When did the doctor tell you this?"

"Two months ago."

Two months? "That seems like a long time to wait. When are you scheduled for surgery?"

"I'm not," she said. "Yet. I had to find someone to come and stay with me first."

I stared at her for a moment, while my brain caught up. I'd assumed that since she was so desperate to get me out here, her procedure was imminent. Who knew how long it would take to get it scheduled? "You realize I can't stay indefinitely, don't you? I have a job to get back to."

"Family is more important," she said imperiously.

"We're not family anymore!" When she stared at me in shock, I said, "Not since your son divorced me. We're not related anymore, Ruth. I told you that on the phone."

"But you're the mother of my grandchildren. I took you in when you were pregnant and had nowhere else to go," she said.

Here comes the revisionist history… "Whatever gave you that idea? My parents wanted me to move back home. I only came here because I was going to marry Gene and Arnie gave him a job."

"I *told* Gene to marry you," she said triumphantly. "He was going to dump you. But I told him no. I said, 'Oh, no, Eugene – that *goy* is carrying my grandchild and you will *not* desert her!'"

"You didn't know I was *goy* 'til after I got here," I said.

She glared at me again. "Anyway," she said, "you're the mother of my grandchildren, and that makes you family. And you have to stay – I've already listed you as my next-of-kin on all the paperwork."

It was my turn to stare at her. "In that case, I need to talk to your doctor. I want to know how long I'm going to have to stay."

She eyed me suspiciously. "Why?"

"Because I have a job, Ruth! And I need to tell them how long I'll be gone, so they don't fire me for not showing up to work!"

"*Hmph.* I suppose so." She unmuted the TV and set down the remote.

I grabbed it and muted the TV again. "Well?"

"Well, what? Turn the sound back on. I want to hear this part."

"When do I get to talk to the doctor?"

She rolled her eyes. "Tomorrow. I have an appointment at ten in the morning." She held out her hand for the remote, and I gave it to her. "Go get your suitcase. I'm too worn out to help you now."

"Fine," I said, and rose.

"You've gotten feisty," she said, and unmuted the TV again.

"You're darn tootin' I have," I said, speaking up to make sure she heard me loud and clear. "And you just wait. You ain't seen nothing yet."

The door to Debbie's childhood room was closed; I opened it and flipped on the light. Nothing appeared to have changed since Gene and I had moved out; Debbie's blue-and-white cheerleading pompons still flanked the mirror above the dresser, and the same faded Holly Hobbie prints hung over the headboard.

I was always surprised that Ruth hadn't redecorated this room after Debbie got married. She had reclaimed Abby's room fast enough, although that made more sense – Abby had covered nearly every inch of wall space with photos of teen heartthrobs and movie posters, and when all that came down, it was clear that the room needed serious repainting. Once Ruth got going in there, she went all the way, ordering one wall painted in a deep hunter green, and a small sofa with green-and-maroon striped upholstery. Then Arnie moved his desk in from the master bedroom and used the space as an office. It made perfect sense, but I never understood why they waited; he could have had a home office years earlier if they'd redone Debbie's room instead of Abby's. It was almost as if Ruth was bent on keeping this room as a shrine.

I unpacked a little. Then I went downstairs to tell Ruth goodnight. She had fallen asleep in the recliner with the TV still blaring.

"Ruth?" I tapped her shoulder, then shook her. "Ruth. Do you want to go upstairs to bed?"

"What?" She started, then struggled to bring the recliner upright. "Who are you? How did you get in?" Then she shook her head. "Oh. It's you."

"Yes, it's me. Maggie. I got here a few hours ago."

"I know that," she said crossly.

"Do you want to go up to bed?" I asked again. "Do you need help getting upstairs?"

"I'm not an invalid," she said, refusing my outstretched hand. "Goodnight." And she shuffled past me to the stairs.

"Welcome home," I muttered to the TV. Then I clicked it off and followed her.

I didn't sleep well, what with the unfamiliar surroundings, and was up before Ruth. I went downstairs in search of coffee, but I didn't see any in the kitchen cabinets – nor did I see the old glass percolator that Ruth had used for as long as I could remember. I contemplated a run to Starbucks, if I could figure out where the closest one was – but just as I was ready to head back upstairs to get my laptop computer, I heard Arnie's old house slippers scuffing along the carpet on the stairs. "Good morning," I called, determined to be pleasant. In the light of morning, I felt a little ashamed of myself for mouthing off to a sick old woman, the way I had the night before. "I was going to make coffee, but I don't see the pot."

"Oh," she muttered, and then she pushed through the saloon-style doors from the dining room. She wore the same getup that she'd had on the night before: pajama pants, oversized robe, and the slippers. "There's a box. In the" – she waved one hand vaguely – "thing."

I followed her hand motions. "In the pantry?"

"Yes." She slid into a chair at the dinette table and groaned.

The groan worried me a little. "Are you okay?"

She waved me off. "Fine. Just hard to get going in the morning." When I still hesitated, she stared at me as if daring me to challenge her. I decided it wasn't worth getting into a fight with her – not until I'd had my coffee, at least. I dropped my shoulders and turned back to the pantry door.

I'd always been a little jealous of Ruth's walk-in pantry. I flipped on the light and gazed around for I wasn't quite sure what. "I don't see…" Then I spied it on the floor: one of those machines that makes one cup of coffee at a time, still in the box. I pulled it out and dusted off the lid. "Is this it? What happened to your percolator?"

"Broke," she said. "Gene bought me that instead, but I've never used it."

I figured Riley was the one responsible for the purchase; Gene had never been much of a gadget guy. I plopped the box on the dinette table and looked for a way in. "It's still sealed," I said. "You've never even had it out of the box?"

"Too confusing," she said. "I want a new percolator. We should get one while you're here."

"But these machines are really easy to use. We have one at work." I slit open the tape on the box lid with a knife and pulled out the packing materials, finally unearthing the machine itself. I took it to the counter and set it next to the sink. "You just fill the tank with water, see? It's even got a handle on the side so you can pull it out and hold it under the faucet. Then you plop a little sealed pod in this drawer here, and hit the start button." I went back to the box and rummaged some more. "They usually give you some pods to start with. Aha!" I pulled out the sample box. "Would you like breakfast blend or hazelnut this morning?"

"What I want," she said grimly, "is a new percolator."

"Well, let's just try this," I said. "Maybe you'll like it better. I'll make breakfast blend for you, and I'll have the dark roast." I rinsed the little tank and filled it, plugged in the machine, and set about making the first cup. The blast of air at the end of the cycle made Ruth flinch, but she took the cup I gave her and sipped at it. "How is it?" I asked.

"Okay," she said. "But I still want a new percolator."

I started my own cup of coffee and eyed her. "What happened to the old one, anyway?"

"I told you. It broke."

"What broke? The handle? The basket for the grounds?"

"The pot, I said!" Then she muttered, "I forgot it was hot and put it in the sink, and it cracked."

I thought about that as I cleaned up the coffeemaker box and its packing material. Then, my own coffee in hand, I sat down at the table with her. "When was this?"

"Right after Arnie died. I wasn't thinking straight." She stared into her cup.

"I can understand that. It must have been stressful."

"You can't imagine." She glanced up at me, her head still down.

"Where was he when he killed himself?" I asked.

Her head came up and she stared at me defiantly. "Now who told you that?"

I met her gaze squarely. "Emmy did."

Her lip curled. "That child is more trouble... Well, she didn't lie to you. He did. He closed up shop early one Friday. Let all of his employees go home. Gave them the afternoon off. And then he went into his office and shot himself in the head." She made a gun of her thumb and forefinger, pointed at her temple, and dropped her thumb as she jerked her head sideways. "Just like that." She dropped her eyes to her cup again. "I wasn't going to tell you, but it figures your kids would blab everything."

I ignored the implied criticism of my child-rearing skills. "Why did he do it?" I asked instead.

She downed the rest of her coffee in one gulp. "I need to get dressed or we'll be late."

Okay, but I'm going to get the whole story out of you before it's over. I gulped my own coffee and put the cups in the sink. Her evasiveness was starting to wear on me. I hoped I'd get some better answers from her doctor.

I'd watched enough medical dramas to believe that all surgeons were young hotshots, so I wasn't prepared for Ruth's surgeon. Dr. Stein seemed like a genuinely nice guy – middle-aged and balding. "You're Mrs. Brandt's daughter?" he asked. "I've heard so much about you."

Oh, really? "Actually, I'm her daughter-in-law," I said, cutting a withering glance at Ruth. "Ex-daughter-in-law, to be more precise."

He laughed at that. "Then you're even more of a saint than I thought," he said. "I can't imagine my son's ex-wife being willing to help me with anything."

"Yeah, well, before last week, I couldn't have imagined it, either." I smiled charmingly at Ruth, who returned the smile with an extra injection of venom. "So, Dr. Stein, maybe you can clear some things up for me. What's the procedure here? How long is her recovery going to take? I need to get back to work at some point."

"The good news is now that you're here, we can proceed. I've already gone over everything with Mrs. Brandt – didn't she tell you?"

"I'm not sure she retained much," I said quietly. "How about you just start at the top."

He looked at Ruth; she appeared to be listening to us, but hadn't reacted to my comment. "Is she hard of hearing?" he asked, just as quietly.

"I'm not sure what I'm up against, to be honest. I just got in last night."

He nodded, sat back, and explained that what she needed was a hysterectomy. "I'll attempt to do it by laparoscopy, which will vastly shorten her recovery time – an overnight hospital stay and then a few days at home, as compared to six weeks of recovery from major abdominal surgery. But as always with a laparoscopic procedure, there's a chance we'll get in there with the camera and discover that it won't work. If so, we'll do it the old-fashioned way. But I don't anticipate any complications."

"So when is the surgery?" I asked.

"How about Wednesday, Mrs. Brandt?" he asked her.

She focused on him with a start. "For what?"

"For your surgery."

"Sure. Let's get it over with."

I shrugged. "I'm good with that."

"All right," he said. "I'll have my nurse set up the appointment. We have some pre-op instructions that we'll send home with you."

"And then what?" I asked. "After the surgery, I mean."

"Well, it depends to some extent on what we find when we get in there," he said. "But I think, given your mother's age, I'll recommend radiation with no chemotherapy."

She's not my mother. I sighed inwardly but didn't correct him. "And how many treatments will she need?"

"Probably one every other week for about two months. She'll need someone to drive her to the appointments."

"Okay, thanks," I said. "I'll talk to my employer and see if they're okay with me taking off that much time."

He gave me a kind smile. "Let me know if my office can do anything to help. We've had plenty of experience with uncooperative employers."

I laughed. "I bet you have."

On the way home, we stopped for an early lunch. By then I was starving – I was used to having at least cereal for breakfast, and this morning I'd had nothing but coffee. "We should stop at the grocery store," I said as we ate. "I need to pick up some milk and cereal. And more coffee pods – we'll run through the sample box in another day or two. And we should get something to make for dinner."

"You don't need to cook for me," she said, picking at her lunch.

"Who said I was going to cook for you?" I meant to be humorous, but it came out more sharply than I'd intended.

"Nobody," she said. "Just don't think you need to do it. I am perfectly capable of cooking my own dinner when I get hungry. I didn't get you out here to take care of me. Just get me back and forth to the doctor's, that's all."

I sighed and wrapped up my burger. "Are you done eating? I can take you home if you don't want to come to the store with me."

"No, I want to come." And she took a bite of her burger almost defiantly. "And anyway, we need to stop at Target and get a new percolator."

My eyes narrowed. "It's starting to sound like there's a bigger story here, Ruth. Did you ask Gene to get you a percolator and he said no?"

She scowled. "Riley said they couldn't find a glass one like I used to have. She said all they have now is metal percolators, and I don't want a metal one. I want what I used to have." She set her lips in a pout. "But she brought over that machine instead."

"Well. I'll take a look online and see if I can't find something for you," I said, thinking that would give me time to stall 'til I could get the other side of the story from Gene. I sighed inwardly. I had been hoping I wouldn't have to see him at all, and now it looked like I would have to actively seek him out. This trip was turning into buckets of fun.

Chapter 4

I awoke from a vivid, troubling dream the next morning to the rattle of my turtle on the nightstand next to the bed.

I had been gliding through the water, sleek and dark and powerful. I hid in the shadows, in the rocks and vegetation along the edges of streams, my feline ears perked to catch signs of the unwary. Fear lined the faces of those who saw me; they screamed and ran away. But many never noticed me, and that pleased me.

I swam just below the surface, my strokes propelling me onward. I enjoyed the game; I lived for it.

Then someone – faces I recognized – tried to pull me from my purpose. They were not afraid, which irritated me. Instead, they were horrified for me, at what I'd become. They tried to reason with me. I was not meant for this, they said. The darkness was too dangerous. It would consume me, and I would be lost to it for all time.

I shrugged them off and swam away. They didn't understand; I had to do this. I had to sink to the very bottom, or I would never be who I was meant to be. They were too late. The woman they knew was already gone; she had been transformed.

I reached for the turtle and pulled it to me. Its vibration slowed, but as I held it, it began to heat up – to the point where I couldn't hold on to it anymore. I set it back on the nightstand in a hurry and blew on my palm to cool it. Then I sat up and rubbed the sleep from my eyes to get a better look at the turtle. Some of the greenish-black patina was gone; along several edges, the original copper shone through. I blinked rapidly. All the elbow grease I'd applied over the years had done nothing, but now the tarnish seemed to be coming off by itself. Maybe the shaking had dislodged it? Or the heat?

And why had it been buzzing just now? My dream felt eerily similar to the vision I'd had in the Great Circle, which made me think they were the same sort of thing: either a past-life regression, or maybe an out-of-body experience. *What do they call those? Astral projections?*

I was going to have to top up my New Age credentials, and quick.

The dream's details were beginning to fade, so I picked up a piece of paper and a pen from Debbie's desk and wrote down as much as I could remember. I wondered what sort of animal I had been. I didn't think I had been a fish, but I didn't know how I came to that conclusion other than that I hadn't felt fish-like. I remembered having paws instead of fins. And I had been conscious as I swam to stay lower in the water than I would have liked, because otherwise my ear tufts would have stuck up above the surface and given my position away.

Ear tufts? On a marine mammal?

And too, I was struck by my own attitude during the dream. The people I came in contact with were scared or dismayed; I was calm, matter-of-fact, and accepting of my nature. Had I been some kind of dark spirit?

I took my laptop with me to the kitchen and did a little research while I ate my cereal. A few moments later, I had a candidate: a water panther. The Ojibwe called it Mishepeshu. It was a variety of monster that lived in deep water in lakes or rivers. The Woodland Indian tribes believed it would lie in wait under ice and drag people down to their deaths.

"Charming," I said aloud, and got up to make a cup of coffee. I decided that if Ruth didn't want to keep the little coffeemaker, I'd take it home with me – it was proving to be a handy gadget. Of course, that would mean getting her a percolator, and *that* would mean having a conversation with Gene to find out why they hadn't just gotten her one in the first place. Because a quick search of my favorite online retailer showed they were still manufactured. In fact, I could have it delivered within two days. No, Gene and Riley must have had some other reason for getting her the pod machine.

Gene and Riley. Every time I thought of them as a couple, my gut clenched. I wondered how she was coping with his penchant for young girls. She couldn't claim she didn't know about it.

That was uncharitable. But it felt good to think it. Maybe I did have a dark side, clamoring to get out.

But a water panther? Nah. That was Gene.

Or maybe his mother.

Nah. She never hid in the shadows. All of her schemes were right out in the open.

The pamphlets Ruth had collected from the surgeon's receptionist were lying on the table. I picked them up and flipped through them: what uterine cancer was, the benefits of laparoscopy, wound care after surgery.

I put them down again and wondered for the hundredth time or so why I was the one stuck with helping her through this. I knew I couldn't stay for the full two months. If I did, I'd lose my job – and if I was going to risk that, it sure wouldn't be in service to someone who had been evil to me for as long as I'd known her. What she needed was a team of helpers, but the organizer was going to have to be someone who hadn't ticked anyone off. At least not recently.

It looked like I was going to need to make a whole lot of phone calls to people I'd rather not talk to.

I glanced out the window at the lightening sky. Still a little early to call anybody in the US, but Tim should be up – and his schedule was the most flexible of anyone's.

I went upstairs to fetch my cell phone and dialed my son's number. If he were still in Europe, it would be midmorning there. Still, I got his voicemail. "Tim, it's Mom," I said. "Your nana is in the middle of a health crisis and you may need to come home to help. Call me. Love you."

Less than a minute later, he called me back. "Sorry I didn't pick up," he said. "I was in the other room and couldn't get to the phone before it went to voicemail."

"That's okay," I said. "I'm just glad to hear your voice."

He ignored that. "Is this about Nana's bogus cancer diagnosis?" he asked instead.

"It's not bogus. I met her surgeon yesterday."

"Wait," he said. "*You're* with her? How did *that* happen?"

"No one else would come," I said.

He paused. "I'm surprised at you, Mom. You don't usually play the martyr."

"Where did *that* come from?" I said. "I'm here because nobody else would come. Or at least, that's what she told me."

"Well, *I* can't come," he said. "I'm teaching English here in Granada now. I wouldn't be able to get home until at least Christmas."

"And Granada would be in…"

"Spain!" he said. "I really love it here, Mom. The people are wonderful – they're so full of *duende* – and the Alhambra is just…" He sighed. "I get to wake up and see it every day. Isn't that awesome?"

"That's wonderful, honey," I said automatically. I had no idea what the Alhambra was, or what *duende* meant. Also, I would have been more enthusiastic if this weren't the third European country my son had fallen in love with. No, fourth: Belgium was first, then France, then Ireland, and now Spain. No, wait – maybe the Netherlands was first, and then Belgium…

"Mom," he said, bringing me back to the present. "I need to go – I have to catch the bus to get to class. You'll have to find someone else to rescue you from Nana's clutches. Sorry."

"You don't sound sorry."

"I'm not, really," he said with a grin in his voice, "but you taught me to be polite."

"Get out of my hair, Timothy," I said. "Love you."

"Love you, too, Mom. Talk soon."

I ended the call with a smile, and set my phone on the nightstand next to my turtle. Only then did I notice Ruth hovering in the doorway. "Good morning," I said.

"Who was that on the phone?" she demanded. "Who were you talking to?

"That was Tim," I said.

"Why did you call him?"

"To chat," I said. "I don't need to give you a reason for my every move."

"Hmm," she said. "Touchy." She moved further into the room, her eyes darting everywhere. Suddenly she snatched up the piece of paper I'd written my dream on. "What's this?"

"Please give it to me," I said, as calmly as I could.

"This was Debbie's," she said. "And you've ruined it!"

My eyes widened. "It was a blank piece of paper, Ruth. I used it to jot down some notes."

"You used her *pen*, too?" she cried.

"Ruth," I said. "Let's go downstairs and get you some breakfast."

"Don't touch *anything* in here!" she yelled. "How many times do I have to *tell* you, Abby?"

"Ruth!" I said, now truly worried. I got off the bed and took her by the shoulders. "Look at me. I'm not Abby – Abby's in California. I'm Maggie. You asked me to come out here and help you through your surgery. Remember?"

She thought about it for a moment. Then she dropped her eyes and muttered, "All these people parading through my house."

That made less sense than her calling me Abby, but I let it go. "You're just stressed out, what with being so sick," I said. "Come on downstairs with me. I'll get you some breakfast." I slid the paper out of her hand and put it on the nightstand. As we headed down the stairs, I realized there were no two ways around it – I was going to have to call Gene.

After breakfast, Ruth settled into the living room recliner with the remote, and I headed out for a walk. I was starting to feel claustrophobic, and anyway, if I was going to have to call my ex-husband, I didn't want to do it where Ruth could overhear.

It was a sunny morning, although chilly enough that I was glad I'd brought my jacket. The leaves had begun to change color, but most had yet to drop from the trees. I walked south along Rock Creek for perhaps a quarter-mile, enjoying the mix of red, yellow, and fading green leaves, and the blue vault of sky beyond them. And I remembered the last real conversation I'd had with Gene.

Did I say *conversation*? I meant *argument*.

I'd just returned from helping my mother in Indiana, and hadn't yet announced that I planned on going back. But he knew. "You're not staying, are you?" he said.

"No," I said.

"Are you sure you want to do this? I can sue you for desertion," he said.

"Whatever it takes to get this sham of a marriage over with."

That clearly was not the response he was expecting. I guess he thought if he threatened me, I'd roll over and do whatever he wanted me to do. He had reason to think so; it had worked for more than twenty years, after all. But that was before I had a life of my own elsewhere. He'd need more firepower now – and he thought he had it. As if revealing his secret weapon, he frowned and said, "Ma's very displeased with you."

Exasperation made me laugh. "Yeah, well, I'm very displeased with her, too. And you can feel free to tell her that." I turned on my heel. "I'll sleep in the spare room."

"Maggie!" he called after me, and I turned. "What can I say to make you believe I'm not an asshole?"

I stared at him. "For starters," I said, "you can stop thinking that what you *say* has any bearing on my opinion of you. You could *do* something, though. That might make me change my mind."

"What?" he asked. "I'll do anything."

"Then do what I've been asking you to do for the past eight years: end the internship program and stop having your little girls on the side."

"They're not little girls," he said.

"That's what I thought you'd say." I turned again to go. "I'll be in the spare room."

"Maggie!" he called again, but this time I kept going.

I hoped our next conversation would have a more pleasant outcome.

I veered off on a side trail where the sound of the creek wouldn't interfere with conversation, found a flat-topped boulder bathed in dappled sunlight, and pulled out my phone. With some trepidation, I dialed Gene's store.

Or at least, I thought I did. "Hello?" the young woman at the other end of the line said.

Terrific. "Is this Riley Brandt?" I asked.

"This is Riley Collingwood," she said, a touch of exasperation in her voice. I imagined she was tired of people not knowing she hadn't changed her name. "Can I help you?"

"I apologize, Riley. This is Maggie. Gene's ex-…"

"I know who you are," she said. "What do you want?"

"I'd like to talk to Gene, if he's there. It's about his mother."

"He's not," she said. "He's at work. You dialed the house."

"I'm sorry," I said again. "I thought I'd dialed the store. Thanks for your help."

"Wait. Maggie." The fight had drained out of her voice. "I'm the one who should apologize. We had an argument this morning before he left. I shouldn't be taking it out on you."

I had no idea why she felt the need to share that with me. Gene's conversations with his current wife were no business of mine. Unless… "Was it about Ruth?"

"Bingo. He's been giving me a hard time for not pitching in more. But honestly, she's just…"

"Horrible."

"Exactly."

"How long has her memory been going?"

She paused. "You want to meet up for coffee?"

All at once, there was nothing I wanted more. She named a place nearby – "they have these amazing croissants" – and I promised to meet here there in half an hour.

It took some time to find the tiny place, tucked into the alley of a strip shopping center. But Riley was right – the croissants were amazing.

"So," I said when we were settled at a table, "Ruth."

"Yeah." She sighed as she doctored her coffee with sugar. I'd never felt that we were competitors – I never took any of his little girls seriously when we were married – but I was surprised at how prickly I felt. She was tiny – not just short, but skinny, with the kind of legs you could cross twice, knee and ankle. She was doing that now as she sat sidesaddle in her chair, twisting at the waist to hunch over her coffee cup.

The coffee reminded me. "What's the deal with the percolator?"

Her mouth twisted, and she looked up at me from under impossibly long lashes. "So," she said, "this was right after Arnie killed himself. You knew that's how he died, right?"

I nodded. "Emily told me."

"Okay. So I get that it would be a shock if your husband offed himself. But she was just, like, a huge *drama queen* about it." She had torn off a piece of croissant as she talked, and now she waved it in a big circle before popping it in her mouth. She chewed for a moment and swallowed before going on. "He was her *life*. She didn't know how she would *go on*. Well, you've met her. You know what she's like."

I nodded again.

"So I thought she was faking it, right? And then she takes the glass coffeepot off the stove – it's literally *full* of coffee; she'd *just* finished making it – and sticks it in the sink. Right on the cold stainless steel. And the pot cracks because it's ancient. I don't care if it's Pyrex or whatever, that stuff doesn't last forever." Her free hand began flailing again. "So now there's coffee everywhere, and she burns herself trying to pour a cup from the *cracked coffeepot* that's *dripping* hot coffee from the bottom, and she calls us, and Gene goes over there and takes her to the emergency room, and he tells me to go to the house and throw the coffeepot away. *Well.* So now she doesn't have a coffeepot, and Gene won't buy her a new one like she had before, because he's afraid she'll break *that* one, *too*. So I got her a machine that takes pods. And she won't use it." She took a hefty bite from her croissant and sat back.

"She's using it now," I said. "I pulled it out of the pantry and set it up for her."

"Good. Gene wouldn't do it."

"Why not?" I asked, surprised.

"He said she had to own her mistake."

I had a flashback, then, of Gene standing over a sobbing Beatrice. Bea couldn't have been more than three or four years old. She was helping me empty the dishwasher when a dinner plate slipped out of her hands and broke when it hit the floor. I hugged her and went to get the dustpan, and while I was gone, Gene came in. He refused to let me clean up the mess; instead he insisted that Bea do it herself. "She needs to own her mistake!" he roared when I tried to intervene. So poor Bea had to pick up the pieces and put them in the dustpan while her father loomed over her. And when, inevitably, she got a shard of ceramic plate stuck in her finger, he yelled at her again and called her clumsy.

I lost it then. I told him to get out of my kitchen and leave my daughter alone. Then I picked up Bea and cuddled her, bandaged her finger, and swept up the rest of the mess myself. But the damage was done.

"I can believe that," I told Riley. "When was this?"

"Just after Arnie died. So maybe a year ago?"

I paused in mid-sip. "I didn't realize his death was that recent."

"Yeah. It wasn't that long ago."

"And now she's fighting cancer." I shook my head. "That's a lot for anybody to process."

"She's just so *mean*," Riley said defensively. "I don't like being around her that much. She makes me feel like a kid."

Well, you are *a kid.* Luckily, I managed to keep my mouth shut. Instead, I said, "She made me feel the same way when we were first married. Makes you wonder what it was like to be raised by her, doesn't it?"

Her eyes grew big. "Wow. I never thought about it that way. Gene and his sisters must have gone through hell."

"The girls both moved far, far away. That ought to tell you something."

"I guess so. I just never…" She shook her head.

"At least they had Arnie to mitigate the damage Ruth did to them," I said. "Gene was very close to his father, but I suppose you know that. I think that's why he turned out relatively okay."

"Yeah. Arnie seemed like a nice man."

"How long have you and Gene been married?"

She eyed me warily. "Three years. Almost four."

Bea had been in middle school when I'd found her father *in flagrante delicto* with Riley, and my daughter was now thirty-one. That made Riley thirty-five or so. Which meant she'd been at least thirty when she met Gene again. I waved a hand. "I'm not accusing you of anything. I'm just trying to get a handle on the timeline. I've been out of touch for some time." I gave her half a grin and took a bite of my croissant.

She relaxed a trifle. "I know your kids, you know. Bea and I talk pretty often."

"How is she?" flew out of my mouth before I could stop myself.

"Good. She's good." She smiled. "And her husband's a good guy. He's Ruth's internist, actually, so you'll probably get to meet him. Seems like she's at the doctor's every other week."

"Old people have a lot going on," I said. "My mom sees her doctor pretty often, too." I paused. "So Bea and her husband are both doctors?"

"Yup. John's an internist, like I said. And Bea's a psychologist, but I guess you knew that part."

"I did." It was Tim who had told me. "Anyway, I should probably tell you the reason I was calling Gene this morning."

The wary look was back. "Why?"

"Her surgeon says the procedure and recovery will take a couple of months, and I just can't be away from home that long. I can't take that much time off work, and I need to be there for my own mother, too."

"That makes sense," she said.

"So I was thinking maybe we could set things up so that her family could take turns with her. That way nobody has to do it all."

"That way nobody has to live with her for two straight months," she said with an arch smile. "I think we can pick up some of the slack. We've been checking on her anyway, since we're the only ones close by. But I need to run it by Gene."

"Of course. Well, this was pleasant. Thanks for suggesting this place."

"You're welcome," she said, and stood. "I'm glad to finally meet you, after everything I've heard about you."

"Am I the monster they've made me out to be?" I said lightly.

"Not at all," she said. I couldn't tell whether she meant that no one had called me a monster, or whether I hadn't lived up to my advance billing.

As we made our way to our cars, I said, "Can I ask you something? Why did you keep your maiden name?"

She smiled a little too brightly. "I thought there were already enough Mrs. Brandts in Gene's family."

Well, then. Advance billing, it was.

Chapter 5

Wednesday morning, dark and early, I knocked on Ruth's bedroom door. "Ruth? It's time to get up and get ready," I said. I'd run this routine for so many years with the kids that I nearly added *to go to school*.

Tim had been the worst to get out of bed. But even at his most difficult, he didn't hold a candle to his nana. "Go away," Ruth mumbled.

"I can't go away. I have to take you to the hospital."

"Not sick."

"Yes, you are. You have uterine cancer, and today the surgeon is going to fix it." I had discovered over the past few days that Ruth's forgetfulness came and went, and usually centered around some truth she didn't want to acknowledge. I'd had to remind her several times why I was staying with her, although she'd never called me Abby again.

"Call them and reschedule," she said. "I'll go tomorrow."

"Tomorrow, the surgeon has other patients to help. It's today or nothing."

"Nothing, then. Just let me die."

That was new. "You don't mean that."

Silence.

I took a chance and opened the door. "Ruth?"

"I'm up," she said from under the covers.

"Don't make me rip that comforter off of you," I said.

She sighed and threw the covers back. "I'm *up*, for God's sake."

"Okay. That's better. We need to leave in half an hour."

"All *right*."

She gave me the silent treatment for the rest of the morning. I was fine with it, as long as she kept moving – which she did. At last, I got her checked in and settled in pre-op, and chatted briefly with the anesthesiologist. Then I went out to the waiting room to hunker down for however long it took.

I had read less than a page of my novel when Gene and Riley came in.

I shouldn't have been surprised, I guess. I'd given Riley the information about Ruth's operation when we met for coffee. But it had never occurred to me that they might show up.

"How is she?" Gene asked me in a low, urgent voice.

"She was fine when I left her," I said. "The anesthetist was with her, and she was dozing off."

"How long did Dr. Stein say it would take?" He sat in the empty chair next to me, his knee against mine.

I moved my leg to give him a little more room. "He said it depends on what they find when they get in there. A few hours, at least. Hi, by the way."

A smile flashed across his face. "Hi. Sorry. I'm a little stressed."

"I can see that. Hi, Riley."

She waved with one hand and gripped Gene's shoulder with the other. It struck me again how tiny she was. She could have rested her chin on the top of his head, seated as he was, without even bending over much.

He looked older. The hooked nose and dark eyes were the same, but he'd gone gray in the nine years since I'd seen him last, and he'd developed a pronounced paunch. Not that I was the skinny kid I'd been in college – I'd lost any hope of returning to my original slim and trim self after baby number three – but I'd watched my own aging in daily increments. Seeing the toll of time all at once was a shock.

Did they look like a couple? Yeah. Did they look like a couple that belonged together? Did it seem like one complemented the other, so that together they were a complete package? No. But I don't think Gene and I ever looked like a complete package, either. Maybe he and Riley would achieve it in time.

"What are you reading?" he asked, pointing to my e-reader.

"Something light," I said. "*Catering Girl* by Laurie Boris. I've been reading a lot of stuff by indie authors lately. You'd be surprised how good they are."

"I might be," he said. "I can't remember the last time I read anything for fun."

"Well, there's no time like the present to start," I said. "You'll have lots of time on your hands today, and there's a little library of paperbacks in the corner." I gestured toward the rack of well-thumbed novels.

He hesitated. "Can we talk about this thing with Ma?"

I glanced between the two of them, and put my e-reader back in my tote bag. "Pull up a chair, Riley," I said. "This may take a while."

When she was situated, Gene said, "Look, I know you're looking for someone to bail you out, but I can't do it right now. I've got the year-end coming, and all our vendors will be on my ass, wanting to be paid."

Riley stared at her husband as if he'd grown a third ear. "She doesn't want us to take *over*, Gene. She wants us to take a *turn*, so she doesn't have to stay *forever*. I *told* you that."

"Still," he said, "it's going to be really busy. I just don't think I can do it."

Riley rolled her eyes. "Well, *I'm* going to do it, and she isn't even *my mother*."

"We're talking two months of medical stuff here," I said. I'd had another discussion with the surgeon about the timetable this morning. "The procedure today, three to four weeks of recovery time, and then three weeks where someone will have to drive her to radiation therapy once a week. You guys could manage the radiation therapy appointments. Those would be just a couple of hours out of your day."

"Sure," Riley said. "We can do that."

"Thanks," I said to her, and meant it. "But we still have a problem, because I cannot stay here for a whole month."

"And what if there are complications?" Gene said. "This is all assuming everything goes well today. What if...?" He looked haunted.

"Stop looking for trouble," I said sharply. "We'll know by the end of the day whether we need to plan for the worst."

He closed his eyes. "Okay. Sorry. Okay. I think I was channeling Ma for a minute there."

"Well, don't," Riley said. "You're freaking me out."

"So who can we tap to take a week or three?" I said. "What about Debbie, or one of her kids?"

Gene snorted. "I don't think Ma would let Debbie in the house."

"Why not? She keeps her room like it's a shrine. I used a piece of paper from the desk in there, and she blew up. You'd have thought I painted 'Jesus Saves' on the wall."

"Oh, my God," said Gene in mock horror. "You should have known better, Maggie."

"Right," I said. "And then while she was scolding me, she called me Abby. How long has she been losing it? Is she seeing anyone for the memory loss?"

Gene's eyes widened. "That wasn't memory loss," he said slowly. "Or, well, it was, but not the way you're thinking of it."

"What was it about, then?"

He looked away. "When we were kids," he said, "Abby went through a phase where she would pull pranks on Deb. She'd short-sheet her bed or hide her homework. Stuff like that. Ma must have been remembering that when she saw you messing with the stuff on Deb's desk."

Riley and I exchanged dubious looks. "Except she didn't see me messing with anything," I said. "She saw that I'd written on a piece of paper with one of Debbie's pens, and accused me of ruining the paper."

Gene shrugged. "I don't know what to tell you. I think I'll check out those paperbacks."

"We're not done," I said, but he got up and left anyway.

"*That* was weird," said Riley. "I'll try to get it out of him later."

"Good luck," I said.

Gene twirled the rack once or twice, selected a book seemingly at random, and rejoined us. "This one looks like it might be okay. So where were we? Right, Debbie helping you out. You can call her, but I don't think she'll do it."

"I think she *needs* to do it," Riley said firmly. "Maggie's already doing more than her share. If Debbie takes a week, Abby takes a week, and *you*" – she poked him in the side – "take a week, then Maggie can go home in a few days and she won't lose her job."

"Unless there are complications," he said.

Riley threw up her hands. "*Fine,*" she said. "We'll discuss it again after we've talked to the surgeon. But you're not getting out of this, Eugene. Not if *I* have anything to say about it." She got up and stalked off.

"Got yourself a feisty one," I offered, as she walked back outside with her arms crossed. "How'd you hook up with her again, anyway?"

"You know, Mags, when the kids say that, they mean it a different way," he said with a sly look.

I shrugged. "In your case, it worked out the same way, didn't it?"

He spread his hands wide and sat back with a smirk. "I suppose it did."

"Well?"

"Well. She brought a load of dry cleaning into the store. We started talking over old times, we went out for a drink, and the rest is history." He leaned forward again and said in a confidential tone, "Turns out she knew I was divorced. She told me she saved up her dry cleaning for months while she got up the nerve to bring it in and talk to me."

"How romantic," I said. "I hope you gave her a discount on her order."

"Well, no. But she gets it for free now." He grinned.

I let him have his moment. Then, matching his tone, I said, "And the interns?"

He looked away again. "I had to discontinue the program. Word started to get around." He looked back at me. "You were right about that, Mags. I should have listened to you. Then maybe we'd still be married."

"But you wouldn't be married to Riley," I said. *And I would have been under your mother's heel for nine more years.* "I think things probably worked out for the best."

He nodded and looked past me, toward the hospital corridor. His eyebrows went up, and he broke into a smile. "John!" he called, rising to shake hands with the new arrival. "Good to see you. I wondered if you'd be stopping by. This is Maggie." He looked meaningfully at me. "John is Ma's doctor."

And Bea's husband. I stood and gave him a hug that he clearly wasn't expecting. "I'm so very glad to meet you," I said. Then I stepped back, beaming, to get a good look at him.

Bea had done well, I thought. John Simms was tall and round-shouldered, as if prone to overcompensate for his height. He wore glasses with plastic frames – trendy, but not too trendy – and a white lab coat, unbuttoned and revealing a sport shirt and slacks underneath. He exuded an air of calm competence. "I'm glad to meet you, too," he said. "I've heard a lot about you."

A number of possible replies sprang to my lips, but none would have made the situation any less awkward, so I simply smiled.

"We should all get together while Mags is in town," Gene said with a broad smile. "Riley and I can have everybody over, once Ma's out of the hospital. Right, Riley?" He held out one arm to his waifish wife as she joined us.

"Sure," she said, evading Gene's hug but taking his hand. "Sounds like a great idea. Hi, John. How are the kids?"

"Doing great. Ryker has finally gotten rid of the cold he had the last time we were over."

"He was *so miserable* that day," said Riley.

"And Royce has a gymnastics demonstration coming up. I'll make sure Bea sends you the date and time, so you can be there."

"Wouldn't miss it," Riley said. And then she looked pointedly at me.

"Oh!" John reddened. "Of course, you're welcome to come, too, Maggie."

"Of course," Gene echoed.

"Of course," I said, as calmly as I could. "I'd love to." And I did want to go. I wanted fiercely to be a part of my grandchildren's lives. I wanted to be a better grandmother to them than Ruth had been to my kids. But I realized the role belonged to Riley.

If only someone had been there when I decided to flee. If only someone had explained exactly what I was giving up, and how my decision would impact the family for generations.

But I hadn't had a fairy grandmother, or a personal adviser from the future. I'd only had my own reasoning ability, and the certainty that I could not spend one more day with my philandering husband and his controlling mother.

"Have you heard anything?" John asked.

"About Ma? Not yet," Gene said.

"I'll see if I can get any information for you," John said, and touched my arm as he left.

Riley watched him go. "*He's* not the roadblock," she said for my benefit.

"Of course he's not," Gene said. "Bea is." He looked at me. "But that's our Bea, right, Mags? That kid always knew her own mind."

"No, she didn't. She did what Ruth told her to do," I said, and then relented. "Sorry. I didn't mean to be so blunt."

"No offense taken," Gene said, and we sat down again to wait.

We made awkward conversation until John came back. "Looks like they're wrapping up. Dr. Stein should be out shortly."

"You're not leaving, are you?" Gene asked.

"Unfortunately, I need to get back to work. I'll check in later." He touched my arm again. "I meant what I said about Royce's gymnastics demonstration. You should be part of the kids' lives, and if I have anything to say about it, you will be."

"Thanks for being in my corner," I said, and hugged him again.

"Sure. See you all later." His lab coat billowed out behind him as he walked away.

"He's a good guy," Gene said.

"Seems like it," I said as I watched him go.

Not long afterward, Dr. Stein found us, and called us into a nondescript consultation room off the waiting room. "She's a trooper," he said. "She came through it very well, and we think we got all of the cancer. No complications."

"Thank God," Gene said, visibly relieved.

"So what does that do to the schedule?" I asked.

"Nothing has changed from what I told you earlier," the surgeon said. "She'll need four to six weeks to heal from the surgery, and then three radiation treatments, one a week."

Gene threw me an impatient look and said, "When can we see her?"

"She's still pretty groggy. Once she's been moved to her room, you can all see her for a moment." And he excused himself, saying he would ask the nurse to let us know Ruth's room number, once she had one.

"What the hell was that about, Maggie?" Gene demanded as soon as the door shut behind the surgeon.

I was still raw from talking with John, or else I would have phrased it better. "I want to go *home*, Gene," I said. "The sooner, the better. The only reason I'm here at all is that neither you nor your sisters could find it in your hearts to be here for your mother. I'm not going to throw away everything I've worked for…"

"Oh, right. 'Everything you've worked for,'" he sneered. "You're working for a casino. That's hardly an uplifting, selfless business, is it?"

"It pays my bills," I said hotly.

"But you're not giving back to the community, are you?"

"You mean the way *you* gave back to the community for all those years?" I hissed. "By seducing…" I glanced at Riley and stopped.

He glanced at her, too, but didn't let up. "Yeah, well, at least I wasn't guilty of causing people to be addicted to anything!"

I laughed. "Oh, like what you did was better?" I turned away from them both. "I can't take this. I need some air."

"You're not staying to see Ma?" he said, incredulous.

"No." And I walked out.

I don't know what I was thinking. Well, I wasn't thinking. All I knew was I had to get away from Gene and his self-righteous bleating. So I walked out the door, went to my car, and left.

But as soon as I got in the car, I realized I didn't have anywhere to go. I could go to a restaurant or a coffee shop, but I didn't want to be surrounded by strangers. And I had no friends here. I hadn't kept in contact with anyone; every woman I'd known was a mother of one of my kids' friends, and as soon as I became the Mother Who Abandoned Her Kids, they disappeared from my life. The only people I was still close to, if you want to call it that, were family. I'd just stalked away from two of them; Bea wasn't talking to me; and the only other one was Ruth.

I sure as heck wasn't going back to Ruth's place. Not right now.

So I drove around for a while: up and down Rockville Pike, past strip shopping center after strip shopping center. I smiled when I saw businesses that were old favorites, and mourned those that were no longer around.

At one point, I cruised past the house where Gene and I had raised the kids. I recognized Riley's car – the one she'd driven to the coffee shop the other day – parked in the driveway, and realized he'd never sold the place. And why would he? The house was paid for, mostly, and it gave the kids stability.

I wondered whether he'd gotten a new bed when he got married again, or whether he and Riley were still sleeping on our old mattress.

That thought gave me the push I needed to wipe my eyes with my sleeve and keep driving, before some nosy neighbor called the cops on me for loitering.

At last, I parked the car on the street near the entrance to Rock Creek Park and got out. A trail meandered down to the creek, and I followed it – but only as far as the first bench I came to. Then I sat, and thought about Gene's parting shot.

How dare he throw my employer in my face? Sure, some people got addicted to gambling. But there were programs to help them. The warnings were prominently posted by the entrances and in the parking garage, complete with the hotline number for counseling. And the casino had turned our little town's economy around – lots of people wouldn't have jobs at all if it weren't for the casino. Including me.

And it wasn't like Gene had never behaved questionably. For a guy who diddled high school girls, he sure had an odd standard of what was moral and what wasn't.

Although a little voice in my head whispered that some might consider my standards suspect, too, even before I moved home and started at the casino. All those years I'd been married to him, pleading with him to cancel the program, I'd never once thought about turning him in. Why was that?

Easy. Because if his reputation were ruined, mine would have been, too. And the kids'. The blowback would have been enormous.

But it would have gotten a child molester off the streets. Because that's what Gene was – a child molester. A pedophile. And I'd let him get away with it.

Out of the corner of my eye, I noticed a turtle on the path. It was moving along at a pretty good clip for a turtle, which I guess is what caught my attention. It crawled off the path to the edge of the creek, and out of nowhere, a midnight black paw – a *paw* – reached up out of the water, snatched the turtle, and disappeared again.

For a moment, I sat there, stunned. Then I got up and walked slowly, carefully, to the creek bank where I'd seen the turtle disappear. Cautiously, I leaned over the water.

There was nothing there. In point of fact, there couldn't have been anything there – the creek was only a couple of inches deep. I knelt and stuck my hand in the cold water, fingers pointing straight down, to confirm it.

And then my copper turtle began to do a dance under my shirt. I clamped my hand over it, and then pulled it out by its chain. More of the tarnish was gone, and the reddish-brown metal that was visible positively gleamed.

I dropped the necklace back inside my shirt and wiped my hand on my slacks. It was time to resume my role in this family that was no longer mine.

Chapter 6

The next couple of days seesawed between duty and boredom. I didn't feel I had standing to stay all day with Ruth at the hospital, despite what she'd told the doctors about me being family. So I would pop in for visiting hours in the morning and evening, and then find myself at sixes and sevens for the rest of the day.

I called my mother every day. She always asked when I was coming home, although she assured me everything was going fine. I had no way to know whether that was true except to call Sandy and Diane, and I didn't want to pester them too often. I didn't want it to look like I didn't trust them.

And I called Ruth's kids. It took me several tries to get through to Debbie; in between leaving her messages, I called Emily to find out the best time to call her aunt Abby. After the usual hemming and hawing about how busy everyone was, I finally got a time frame out of my daughter, and told her specifically not to tell Abby I was planning to call. I had visions of Abby dodging me.

"Stop being ridiculous," Em said. "You make her sound like a fugitive from justice."

"Isn't she?" I said. "Why is it that I'm here and she's not?"

"Because you still can't tell Nana no," she said with a snort.

I resisted the urge to deliver a withering comeback, and instead said, "And how are you doing? Classes going well?"

"Pretty well. Either my students this semester aren't as thick-headed as in previous years, or I'm getting better at this teaching thing."

"Option B, of course. And your research? How is that going?"

"Really well. I've had a paper accepted for publication, which will make me look really good to the Ph.D. programs I'm applying to."

"Wonderful!" I didn't press her for details, and she didn't offer. We both knew I would have no clue about what she was studying. After we all got over the shock of her stellar SAT performance, her high school counselor pulled her aside and talked up STEM careers to her. And Em, who still didn't much care for any academic discipline in particular, decided she might as well go for it. Then she got to college and absolutely fell in love with computer architecture, or whatever it's called. Designing systems, anyway, I think. The point was that once she had her degree, she could get a job in any number of industries and do very well financially – and at the same time, she would be rebelling against her nana's belief that she was an airy-fairy artist of some kind.

At the appointed hour, I dialed Abby's number and a woman whose voice I didn't recognize answered the phone. "Is this Abby Brandt?" I asked.

"No," she said crisply.

"Well, is Abby there?"

"Whom shall I say is calling?"

Who is this woman, anyway? "Tell her it's Maggie."

"Just a moment." The woman had a short conversation in low tones with someone, and then Abby's deep, cigarette-roughened voice came on the line. "Holy shit, Maggie," she said. "After all these years."

"Yeah, sorry. I haven't been the best correspondent," I said.

"No, that's not what I meant. It's totally understandable that you wrote us all off. What I meant was, 'Holy shit. It's good to hear from you.'"

I smiled. "It's good to hear your voice, Abby." Of Ruth and Arnie's three kids, I'd liked Abby the best. Better than Gene, even. He was just my husband; Abby and I bonded.

"Oh, wait. This isn't just a call for old times' sake, is it?" She sighed. "How's Ma doing?"

"Okay. She had the surgery a couple of days ago and the doc said it went well. She's going to need to take it easy for a few weeks, though, while she heals. And then she needs to go for weekly radiology sessions for a few weeks."

"And you're looking to share the wealth."

"Kind of, yeah." I grinned weakly. "Seriously, Abby, I can't stay for two months. My mom isn't in the best of health, either, and I'm all she has."

"I can't believe you went out there at all," she said. "Ma really must be scraping the bottom of the barrel to have called *you*. You wouldn't believe the stuff she said about you after you left."

"Yeah, I would," I said. "I expect she said most of it to my face while I was packing." That last day had been horrible. Ruth had showed up on our doorstep to rail at me about what a lousy, rotten wife and mother I was. I had locked the door in anticipation of her appearance, but it did no good; she let herself in with her copy of our house key.

"That sounds like her." She let out a breath. "Hang on a sec." She covered the mouthpiece and had another quiet conversation with the same woman who had answered the phone. Then she came back on the line. "Yeah, okay. I think we can swing a week."

We? "That's great. Thanks so much, Abby. Um, I don't mean to be nosy, but…"

"Emmy didn't tell you?"

"I guess not, since I'm asking."

I could hear her grinning. "I got married six months ago."

"Congratulations!" I said. "Who's the lucky guy?"

"Uh, well, it's a lucky *woman*. Sallie. You just talked to her."

"Oh!" I could feel my face flushing. "Sorry. It's just…I had no idea."

"Surprise, surprise," she said drily. "Here." And she handed the phone over to her bride.

"Congratulations to you, too," I said. "Nice to meet you over the phone."

Sallie laughed. "Same here. So you're the one who abandoned Emily?"

She'd said it lightly, but it still didn't set right with me, coming from someone who'd never met me. Still, I tried to laugh it off. "There were extenuating circumstances," I said, in what I hoped was a pleasant tone of voice.

"Oh, sure. Of course. I didn't mean to imply…" She trailed off. "Boy, I stuck my foot in it, didn't I? Will you forgive me?"

"Sallie," I said, "if you can get your wife out here to take over from me for a week, I'll be your best friend forever. Have you met Ruth?"

"Nope. She doesn't exactly approve of women marrying other women."

"Well, consider yourself lucky." That got a laugh. "Listen, I've got to run. Nice to talk to you."

"And to you, as well. Here's Abby."

The phone was passed back, and Abby said, "You're not mad, are you?"

"Of course not," I kind of lied. "But if you don't get your butt out here in a couple of weeks, I might be."

With Abby and Riley on board, that left just one sibling – and I suspected she would give me the most trouble. I was right.

"I just can't see how I could get away right now," Debbie said, smooth as silk. She'd picked up the tiniest bit of a Southern accent, which shouldn't have surprised me. She had attended Tulane and met her husband, Aaron Schmidt, there. He was another East Coast refugee; his parents had come to the Gulf Coast to help with the cleanup from Hurricane Camille and never went home. Debbie did me one better by actually finishing her degree, in Jewish studies. Gene said she had planned to go on to law school, but it had never happened; instead, she went to work to support Aaron while he earned his doctorate in optometry, and then she stayed home and raised their four children, all of whom were grown. Our kids were all in the same range of ages, but the cousins had only met a couple of times. As a store manager, it was hard for Gene to get away, and Debbie appeared to have zero interest in seeing her parents.

"I hear you," I said. "We all have busy lives. But Riley and Gene are going to handle the radiology treatment weeks, and Abby's going to come for a week."

"Is she," Debbie drawled. "Is she bringing that woman she married?"

"I have no idea," I said. "I only just learned she'd gotten married. Have you met Sallie?"

"No," she said, in a tone that said she had no interest in ever meeting her.

I plowed on anyway. "She seemed nice on the phone," I said. Then, with a short laugh, I said, "I was a little bit shocked to find out that Abby was gay, though. Did you know that?"

"She's bisexual," Debbie said.

"Ah. So you did know before she married Sallie?"

"No," she said. "Look, it's been lovely to chat with you, but I have an appointment that I really must not miss. I'll talk with Aaron tonight, but I really don't think we can swing it."

"All right," I said. "I understand. I'll call you again tomorrow."

"No need," she said. "If my answer changes, I'll call *you*."

So back I went to Abby. "Why is she so resistant to coming home?" I asked. "You must have some clue."

For a few moments, Abby was silent. Then she said, "She's still mad at Ma. Something happened when we were teenagers, and Ma took it out on Deb. She's never forgiven her for that."

"Is that why Debbie's room is frozen in time?"

Abby laughed. "That's a good way to put it. Yeah, that's why. Ma didn't want to change anything – she wanted to make it clear that it wasn't her fault that Deb left."

"Which means it was."

"Oh, yeah." She paused. "Well, there was plenty of blame to go around. But Ma had her part in it, that's for sure."

"Abby?" I said. "What happened? Why did Debbie feel like she had to leave?"

Again, she paused. The silence grew.

"Abby?" I said. "Are you still there?"

"Yeah," she said. "I'm just debating about what I should say." Another pause. "Nope. I don't think I should be the one to say it. You need to ask Gene."

"Gene?" I said in surprise. "I don't know if you've noticed, but we're divorced. He's not going to tell me anything."

"Well, it's his secret to tell," she said. "His and Deb's. Sorry."

I realized I was clenching the fist that wasn't holding the cell phone. I opened my hand and stretched the fingers as I took a deep breath and let it out. "It's okay. Sorry to be nosy."

"It's not being nosy when it's family," she said. "And like it or not, Maggie, you're still family."

"I'm finding that out," I said. "So you're still coming for a week, right?"

"I suppose you want me to make it two, now, don't you? Since Deb turkeyed on us."

"I wasn't going to ask. But if you're offering, I won't turn you down."

"Let me talk to Sallie. I had just about gotten her talked into a week with Ma. I'm not sure how she'll feel about doubling her exposure." She giggled. "Sallie calls her the Mother of Dragons."

I thought about Ruth's children: imperious Debbie; Gene, who believed the bounds of propriety didn't apply to him; and Abby, who was just as headstrong as her siblings, but in her own way. "She's got a point," I said.

I had one more call to make: to my boss. I'd left my return date pretty open-ended, and even though I didn't know a great deal more than

I had when I left work the week before, I wanted to give them as much of an update as I could.

Delancey answered the phone with his standard, "Yello."

"Hi, Dee, it's Maggie."

"Long time no see," he said sarcastically.

"Yeah, I know." I took a breath: in, out. Sometimes the best way to manage the guy was to butter him up. For sure, getting upset wouldn't work. "I want to thank you again for letting me take this time off."

"You know you're not getting paid for it, right? You used up all your vacation days before you decided to go off on this little jaunt," he said.

"I'm aware of that," I said in my best professional tone of voice. "You were very clear on that point when we discussed this before I left."

"Well, okay. Just so we're clear."

"Yes, we are."

"Okay. So what can I do you for today?"

I obliged him with a laugh, hoping it didn't sound phony. The joke had long since stopped being funny. "I just wanted to let you know my approximate timetable for returning. I know we left it pretty open-ended."

"Right. So when can I put you back on the schedule?"

"Well," I said, "Ruth came through the surgery fine. But the doctor says she needs to recuperate for four to six weeks."

"Six weeks?" he spluttered. "That's too long! I can spare you another week, maybe, but not any longer than that. We need to get busy on paying the vendors so we can close the books for the year on time."

"I can't do a week. I need at least two. I've got someone coming to spell me then, but I can't leave any sooner than that."

"I guess I can make two weeks work," he said ungraciously. "But you make sure to get your butt back here in two weeks, okay? I don't know that I can hold your job open any longer than that. Corporate will be on my back about it as it is."

"Two weeks. Got it," I said. "Thanks, Dee. I owe you."

"Yeah, yeah. Two weeks." And he hung up.

I ended the call and sat back, somewhat relieved. If Abby could take the last two weeks of Ruth's convalescence, everything would work out. If she could only stay a week, I was pretty sure Riley would be willing to pick up the second week. So I should only have another week and a half here, and then I could go home. I could survive that long.

If Ruth didn't heal as quickly as we hoped, or if some complication popped up, then of course the schedule would fall apart. But I couldn't contemplate that now. I was determined to think positive thoughts. Otherwise I might lose it completely – and I had to hold it together. For Ruth, of all people.

Chapter 7

The next day, I brought her home. She was so cranky that I was tempted to give her the maximum dosage of pain medication, just to knock her out. But I didn't want to run the risk of adding "hooked ex-mother-in-law on opioids" to my list of sins, so I stuck to the minimum dose and only gave her more when she asked for it.

She hadn't said anything more about wanting to die, so I chalked up that one comment to pre-surgery jitters. Also, she never called me by anyone else's name again – but then, I'd instituted a strict hands-off policy in Debbie's room regarding anything that I hadn't brought with me from home.

I tried to stick to the same policy everywhere else in the house. When I cooked, whether for both of us or for just myself, I made sure I bought fresh ingredients. It was a strain on my budget – food prices were higher on the East Coast than they were at home, and I wasn't used to feeding two people – but again, I didn't want to run the risk of someone accusing me of somehow taking advantage of Ruth.

Although how that could happen, considering she'd asked me to come after all of her kids had turned her down, I didn't know. But people who want to accuse you of something will always find a reason for it. At least, that's been my experience.

I did ask her about Debbie's room. "How come you never remodeled in there?" I said.

"Why should I?"

"Well, I don't know. Maybe to have a proper guest room, since that's what you seem to use it for."

"Nobody stays in there but family," she said.

"But still," I said. And then I shut up and waited.

"I want Debbie to feel welcome when she comes home. I don't want her to feel like I don't love her," she said. Keep in mind that she was talking about a woman who hadn't set foot in the house for thirty years.

"But you didn't waste any time remodeling Abby's room when she moved out," I said.

"I didn't care if *she* left," Ruth said.

I opened my mouth to say something else, and then closed it again. For it suddenly dawned on me that they'd never redone Gene's room in the basement, either. "Did Gene always have that room in the basement?" I asked. "Even when he was little?"

"Of course not," said Ruth. "You know he didn't."

I didn't know anything of the sort. I wondered who she thought she was talking to now. But I let her ramble.

"No, the girls shared a room and Gene had his own room. You remember."

"Sure," I said, "but I don't remember which was which."

"The girls were next to us…"

"In Debbie's room?"

"Yes," she said. "And Eugene was down the hall. It wasn't until…" She lapsed into silence.

"Until what?" I prodded.

She looked sharply at me. "I'm hungry," she said. "When's lunch?"

I let her get away with it. But I continued to think about it, the way you might worry an abscessed tooth with your tongue: it's probably not a good idea, but it doesn't really hurt, and it gives you something to do to pass the time.

I'd always believed that the girls had moved far away from home because of Ruth's stellar mothering style. But this was starting to sound like something else. Obviously Ruth missed Debbie terribly, but Debbie wouldn't give her the satisfaction of coming home. Ruth didn't care whether Abby came home or not, and that didn't seem to faze Abby – so either she didn't know, or she knew and didn't care. Or she knew, and was lying to herself about how much she cared. Or she knew, and was putting up a false front to hide her pain from the world.

And somehow Gene was involved. Something dire happened when the kids were teenagers – something that forced Gene down to the basement, almost as if he'd been banished, and split up the girls in separate rooms. Knowing my ex-husband's preference for sweet young things, I wondered whether he'd been messing around with his sisters, but that seemed too obvious. Although if Debbie had caught Gene and Abby in their shared room, say...and then Ruth defended Gene, or refused to take her complaints seriously, or something...and then Debbie insisted on having her own room, so Gene was sent to the basement/dungeon...

And let's not forget that Arnie killed himself over some shadowy thing that no one wanted to talk about. What if it wasn't money laundering? What if he, too, had been covering for Gene all these years, and someone threatened him with exposure?

I was beginning to think this suburban split-level should have been one of those creepy old Victorian houses, with hidden staircases and a ghost in every moldy closet.

But even while I was entertaining myself by spinning these yarns, I knew I was really just looking for vindication. I wanted God or the neighbors or *somebody* to confirm that I'd done the right thing by getting out. Because it hadn't escaped my notice that my relationships with my own kids followed much the same patterns as in Gene's family of origin: Bea had broken ties with me, as Debbie had with her mother; Emmy stayed in contact with everyone, just like Abby; and Tim – well, there's where the comparison broke down. Because Gene had dutifully moved home and joined the family business, whereas Tim appeared inclined to stay the farthest away of all my kids.

And too, none of my kids were gay – unless there was something somebody wasn't telling me. And that made me wonder how much Ruth knew.

So I brought it up. "I hear Abby's married now," I said at dinner one night, several days after she'd returned home, and waited for her reaction.

"You mean she's shacking up with that dyke," Ruth said with a snort.

Okay, then. "No, they're actually married. You know it's legal in all fifty states now, don't you? The Supreme Court said so in June. But California legalized it much earlier."

She blew a raspberry. "If you say so."

That put a slightly different spin on things. Ruth may have stopped caring much more recently about whether Abby came home. Although if that was true, it didn't fit so well with my remodeling theory.

I was beginning to wish I had something else to think about.

And then I did. Riley invited us all to a get-together at their place – Bea and her husband and kids, Ruth, and me. "It'll be sort of an early Thanksgiving," Riley said when she called, "since you'll be on your way home by then."

"I sure hope so," I said. I still hadn't gotten a firm arrival date out of Abby, and it was starting to make me nervous. "Anyway, what can we bring?"

"Just yourselves," she said. "I'm taking care of everything."

"She always says that," Ruth said. "And everyone always brings something anyway. I took her at her word once. Once! And Arnie and I were the only ones who came empty-handed. I felt like such a schmuck. Never again, I'm telling you. We're bringing something, even if it's only a bottle of wine."

So I purchased a couple of bottles of wine on my next trip to Wegman's. Ruth didn't go with me to the store – she was still a little too shaky on her pins, she said, even though the doctor had said walking would do her good. But after I got back, when she saw me take the wine out of the bag, she said crossly, "What are you doing, buying wine?"

I paused in the act of setting the bottle of cabernet on the kitchen table. "You said we should get some to take to the party."

"No," she said with exaggerated patience. "I said we should *bring* some. I never said we should *buy* some." At my confused look, she said, "There's a whole wine rack in the basement, just full of the stuff. Arnie started collecting it toward the end. Go see." She shooed me away from the table and toward the basement stairs, which were near the back door.

I put one foot on the first step. Then I turned toward her. "Are you sure you're okay with this? I mean, if it was special to Arnie…"

"*He's* not gonna drink it. And I'm not gonna, either. You know I've never been a big drinker. I'd never finish half of what's down there."

I shrugged and descended the stairs, flipping on lights as I went. It had been years since I'd been down there. I still thought of the basement as Gene's territory; I'd been in his old room only once or twice, and I'd never had to sleep there. Back then, the rest of the basement had been unfinished. I remembered it as a utilitarian space where the washer-dryer and several rusty kids' bikes resided, along with shelves of partial cans of paint and other remnants of past home-improvement projects. There had been an exterior door, too, that opened onto the backyard. Gene had joked about how convenient that entrance was during his teen years, on the occasions when he'd stayed out past curfew.

I'd always thought that walk-out basement was a wasted opportunity; it could have been a nice indoor/outdoor space with a little sprucing up. So I was pleasantly surprised to discover that sometime in the past nine years, someone had done my idea one better: lovely French doors had been installed where the single-light door I remembered had been. Beyond, I could see the frumpy concrete patio was gone, replaced by terra cotta pavers. Moreover, the basement had been carpeted, and partition walls enclosed a pleasant room kitted out for entertaining, with a wet bar, a comfy-looking sofa and chairs, and the aforementioned wine rack that took up the whole wall behind the bar.

I stepped to the door and gazed around the backyard – and remembered suddenly the last time I'd been out there, for Emmy's high school graduation party.

My father had died that spring, and when we went back to Indiana for the funeral, we could all see that my mother was having trouble coping. So I offered to come back out and stay with her for a few weeks, to help her get the paperwork sorted out. I planned to leave Maryland right after Emmy's high school commencement and be back by mid-August, in time to see the girls off to college. At least, that was the public timetable.

Bea was consumed with med school applications and Tim was in the middle of lacrosse playoffs. Gene, too, was distracted, by his latest young intern. Only Emily was paying attention. "Seriously, Mom," she said. "Don't come back."

"I may not," I admitted. "Don't tell Nana."

Emmy rolled her eyes. "She already knows."

She was right, of course. Ruth had been giving me the evil eye ever since we got back from my father's funeral. I'd been avoiding her as much as possible – the end of the school year was always busy, but senior year was the worst, what with prom and post-prom, the last this and the last that – but we finally had it out during that graduation party.

I hadn't wanted a party, and Emmy hadn't, either. But of course, Ruth wanted a big shindig of the sort we'd had when Bea graduated. She'd begun hinting about party planning at Thanksgiving, and I'd been putting her off. Now, at last, I thought I had an ironclad excuse. "We're in mourning, Ma," I said. "Emily just wants a sleepover with her friends, and to be honest, that's all I have the energy for."

"I know, dear," Ruth said, patting my hand. "You've been through a lot. Just leave everything to me."

"Oh, no. I couldn't let you do that," I said, even though I knew my protest would be futile. If she wouldn't cave to grief, she wasn't going to cave just because I said no.

"It's no bother," said Ruth. "And we can't disappoint the family. They'll be so upset if they can't come to congratulate dear Emily."

"They could just send a card," I said, thinking of all the condolence cards I hadn't received from Gene's side of the family when my father died.

"Nonsense," Ruth said. "It'll be fun. You'll see."

What I saw was the bill from the caterer, which included the date on the initial contract. Ruth hadn't pulled this thing together at the last minute. She'd been setting it up for the last six months.

I snatched up the bill from the kitchen island and went outside to find her. She was standing in a circle, chatting up some of Montgomery County's elite; these parties always featured more of Arnie's business contacts than family, so the Brandts could use them as a tax write-off. "A moment," I said to Ruth, touching her arm.

She excused herself with a smile, then preceded me to a spot by the fence. She turned to me with an annoyed look and said, "Couldn't you see I was busy?"

I shook the catering bill at her and hissed, "When were you going to tell me that we were having a party, whether Emily wanted one or not?"

"When are *you* going to admit that you're leaving my son?" she countered.

Automatically, I looked around. "Keep your voice down," I said.

"Don't you dare tell me what to do!" she yelled, and now people *were* looking our way. "After all I've done for you – welcoming you into the family, giving you a home, introducing you to the best families in D.C., throwing parties for you – you would raise your voice to me?"

"You're the one whose voice is raised," I said, striving to keep my tone level.

"After all we've done for you!" she went on. "After all my son has done for you!"

"After all your son has done *to* me!" I said, without thinking.

"Oh, fine! Drag his name through the mud to make yourself look better!" she said. "You shrew!" And she lunged for me.

Thank God Arnie stepped in and grabbed her wrists. "That's enough," he said.

"Did you hear what she said to me?" she cried.

"I said, that's enough." He threw me a glance – half disgusted, half mortified – and led her away, into the house.

People nearby were still eyeing me speculatively. I stared them all down until they turned away. Then I caught sight of Gene, standing near the open bar with a gaggle of Emmy's friends around him. His look was cold. Calculating. Challenging.

I went home and packed. I pulled my turtle from its hiding place and put it on reverently, as if it were a talisman that would protect me and mine from all harm. Then I got in the car and drove away.

I contemplated leaving notes for each of the kids, but I had an irrational fear that Gene – or Ruth – would find them first and throw them away. So instead, I emailed them from the road. *I'm so sorry*, I said to each of them. *I love you. I miss you already. I just couldn't take it anymore.*

Don't sweat it, Tim wrote back. *See you in August.*

Emmy said, *Don't apologize. You did what you had to do.*

Bea didn't respond at all.

Stuck in my reverie, I wheeled in surprise when Ruth spoke up behind me. I hadn't realized she'd followed me down the stairs. It took me a few seconds to reconcile the snarling, vital woman I'd just been seeing in my mind with this frowzy, older version.

"I guess it was after you left that we did all this," she said. "I kept telling Arnie that I wanted to start entertaining more. Finally, he said okay, and we hired the contractor and got it done. And it worked great." She sunk into one of the easy chairs, and I perched on the edge of the other one. "We had couples over almost every weekend to play cards and drink. It was mostly business-related, you know, so we could write it off on our taxes. But I'd always invite somebody we knew from temple, and a neighbor or two." She closed her eyes and smiled. "Oh, we had some good times."

"Why did you stop?" I asked.

Her smile faded. "I don't know."

"How long ago?"

"How long ago was the last party?" She thought about it for a moment. "Sometime before Arnie died. Maybe six months before. He didn't feel like doing much of anything toward the end." Her mouth curled up in disgust. "And people weren't reciprocating, anyway. We only got a handful of invitations from people we'd invited over. I had to be the hostess with the mostest to have any kind of social life at all. And after Arnie died – poof!" She flicked the fingers of one hand wide. "That was it. Nobody brought over so much as a casserole." She tugged her bathrobe more tightly around her.

"Death is a hard thing for people to cope with," I said. "They don't know what to say or what to do. They're afraid to say the wrong thing, or they think anything they say will be taken the wrong way. And suicide makes it worse."

She nodded as she fiddled with an end of the bathrobe's belt. "Well, it won't matter anyway in a while. None of it will matter."

"Oh? What makes you say that?"

She looked up at me, calm acceptance in her eyes. "Because I'm gonna die soon."

Here we go... "What makes you say that?" I said carefully. "The surgeon said he got all the cancer."

"He *thinks* he got it all," she said. "That's what the radiation is for – to try to kill anything he missed." She closed one eye and shook a finger at me. "You thought I wasn't paying attention to what he said, didn't you? Well, you were wrong."

I had wondered how much of the guy's words had registered; she'd had her eyes closed for most of the time I chatted with him. "Okay," I said, "I was wrong. But that doesn't mean you're going to die soon. The whole idea is to keep you alive."

She gave me a skeptical look and glanced away. Then she said, "You can have the house."

"What?"

"I'm giving you the house, Maggie. *This* house."

"Why?" I blurted.

"Because you've been better to me than my own kids," she said. And to my further surprise, she began to cry. "I know I've been a rotten mother to them," she said, wiping her eyes with her bathrobe sleeve, "and I was a rotten wife to Arnie. He left me by his own hand, and none of the kids are speaking to me."

"What are you talking about?" I said. "Gene's talking to you. We're going to his house for a party. And you talked to Abby on the phone just last week."

"But they're not *really* talking to me. Not the way they did when they were little." She sniffed. "They don't tell me their secrets anymore."

"Well, that's how it works," I said, remembering the days when my own kids told me their secrets. We had all been so young back then. "You raise them to be adults," I went on, "and then they go off and do adult things. And they don't always want to share those things with their mothers. I'm sure you kept stuff secret from your own mother, didn't you?"

She giggled and wiped her face with her sleeve again. "And how. You wouldn't believe half the things I kept from her."

"See? That's what I mean. That's the way of the world."

She nodded, and patted her damp sleeve. "I suppose you're right." Then she gave me a crafty look. "But I'm still giving you the house. I'm calling the lawyer in the morning."

"Ruth, please don't," I said. "I wouldn't have any use for it. I don't live here anymore."

"What did you think of that doctor?" she said suddenly.

I blinked. "Which one? Your surgeon?"

"Yeah. Dr. Stein. He's kind of cute, don't you think?"

Now where did that *come from?* "I hadn't thought about it, to be honest. Why?"

"I happen to know he's single," she said. "And doctors make a good living."

I couldn't help but laugh at her. "Are you trying to fix me up with your surgeon?"

"Why not?" she said. "A girl's got to think about her future when she gets to be a certain age. You two are about the same age, wouldn't you say?"

I pictured the guy: middle-aged, balding, average build. Nice hands. "Just stop," I said, as much to myself as to her. "We don't have anything in common."

"How do you know? You haven't even spoken to him, except to talk about me!" She extracted a business card from her bathrobe pocket. "You should call him. Ask him out for lunch or something."

I looked at the business card she waved at me. "You're serious, aren't you?"

"Take the card, Maggie," she ordered.

I took it and slipped it into my own pocket. I had a vague plan to leave it there until after the slacks went through the wash. *Oh, darn. I guess I can't call him now...*

"I want to see you settled," she said. "It breaks my heart to see your life in such a mess."

"So you're going to give me a house and marry me off, is that it? I appreciate your concern, but really, Ruth, I'm fine."

"So you say," she said. "Just keep the card." She shook her finger at me again. "And call him. I'm going to keep after you until you do it."

Terrific. My very own Jewish matchmaker. "Let me take a look at the wine wall here, and see if any of this stuff is better than what I bought today," I said.

Arnie, it turned out, had had very good taste – or at least, very expensive taste. I didn't know anything about wine, but a quick web search told me he'd spent a lot of money building his collection. "Are you sure it's okay if we drink this stuff?" I asked her at one point. "Some of them are going for hundreds of dollars apiece."

"Put that thing away," she said, pointing at my laptop. She waited until I'd shut down the device. Then she said, "Learn to accept a gift," and turned away.

Speechless, I glared at her back as she shuffled off. Everything she'd said to me that day – every criticism, veiled and not-so-veiled – came back to me in a rush. How dare she tell me how to live my life? Who was she to judge whether I needed to own a house? To date a doctor? To live the way she thought was best? How presumptuous of her – and how very typical. She ran down the choices of everyone she cared for, critiquing and criticizing, until their self-esteem plummeted and they felt the only way to be themselves was to stop listening to her.

And where did she get off, anyway, telling me I didn't know how to accept a gift? What if the gift was all wrong for me? What if I didn't want it? What if I'd never asked for it?

Then I heard a voice in my head: *What if the gift is something you didn't know you needed? What if it's the one thing that will make your life perfect, but you turn your back on it because of the person who has offered it to you?*

Only then did I feel my turtle necklace vibrating. I glanced after Ruth, making sure she was really gone, and then pulled the necklace from its accustomed spot under my shirt. The turtle stopped moving as soon as I touched it, and now it lay inert on my palm. Its patchy patina hadn't changed this time – in fact, it looked a little less shiny than when I'd put it on that morning.

Was I hallucinating? Had it spoken to me, or had the voice been that of my own better self? Or had it been Granny? Because the more I thought about it, the more the mysterious voice sounded like hers.

She had said three doors would close to me, and I would close three more. Was my stubbornness liable to cut me off from something that would benefit me?

It sure seemed like that was the message the turtle had for me – either the turtle, or whoever had given it to me in that past life and then placed it in my way in this one. The last time the necklace had been this excited, I was sitting near the creek and thinking about the ethics of working at the casino – and then watched as the water panther snatched a turtle from the bank. Before that, it woke me from the dream in which I was the water panther. And before that, it had buzzed wildly as I approached the Great Circle – right before I remembered the ceremony in which I'd received the turtle the first time, and then met Granny and Zed.

I began to believe the real mystery here had nothing to do with whatever had happened in this house when the Brandt kids were teenagers. It seemed to have more to do with me.

What had Granny said? *It is only by humanity's renewal that the Earth itself may be renewed.* Yes, that was it. So I was supposed to remake myself, and that's what all this business about doors closing and opening was about.

A fragment of that ancient ceremony came back to me – not verbally, because I still didn't understand the shaman's language, but emotionally. I felt sure he had told me I was the turtle – the essence of the Turtle Island we lived on and had been born from.

The markings on its back were a map. A sky map. And they showed the path of the moon from major to minor standstills. I was supposed to do something to guide the people along that path…

The turtle grew warm in my hand, and a bit more of the patina melted away.

Had I not done my job back then? Or had I been successful, and so that's why I was chosen in this incarnation to do it again?

It would have been really useful to have Granny to talk to just then. I had a whole bunch of questions for her – although I wasn't sure she would have been able to answer them. She believed herself to be a Shawnee spirit, not a Hopewell one. In fact, nobody knew anything about the Hopewell's cosmogony – all anthropologists had to go on were grave goods and the alignments of the various heavenly bodies with the edges and corners of their ceremonial earthworks. Even with Granny's help and advice, it's likely I would be on my own.

And then I chided myself for my hubris. Why, I was starting to sound like I believed all this stuff. Wasn't there some mental condition in which the sufferer believed they were specially chosen to do something grand? Megalomania or something, wasn't it?

I mean, I didn't feel like I was crazy. But they say the really crazy people never think they are; if you can conceive of the possibility that you're nuts, then you're probably okay.

Probably. It was that qualifier that made me stuff the turtle back under my shirt and set aside my questions in favor of getting ready for the party at Gene's.

I helped Ruth get into the shower, and also helped her out when she was done. She was as cranky as ever, but I realized it was mostly because she needed the help at all; she wasn't angry with me so much as she was angry at the situation, and that made her mood easier for me to bear.

As I left her alone to dress herself, I thought of something that had gotten by me earlier: Ruth saved her choicest criticism for people she cared about. It was a twisted way of showing love, no two ways about it. But it meant that in offering me her house and demanding that I take her dating advice, she was demonstrating that she loved me.

My ex-mother-in-law loved me. Now there was a weird concept to wrap my brain around. I was going to have to work on accepting it. It still seemed more likely that she was trying to take care of me because she felt bad for the way her son had treated me.

How much, I wondered, had she known about what went on between Gene and his interns?

And there I was, back to the mystery of Debbie's bedroom.

I was standing in that very room when my brain circled onto its familiar track. I'd closed the door for privacy while I dressed for the party, and now I took the opportunity to look around with fresh eyes.

Debbie would have been eighteen when she left for college, but many of the furnishings – the bed, the books on the shelf, even the clothes in the closet – seemed to be geared toward a younger girl. Granted, if she'd had this room since she was tiny, it would still feature a lot of little-kid stuff in the nooks and corners. But I didn't see much of anything from her high school career. I thought Gene had told me his older sister had been a cheerleader. Her pompons were on the wall, but where were the flirty skirt and the letter sweater? High school yearbooks? Mementos from senior prom? Didn't kids in Maryland collect all that junk the way we had in Indiana?

I pulled a box at random from the hutch above the desk and opened it. Here, at last, were some of the mementos I had expected to see: football ticket stubs printed in orange and black, a stuffed toy ram, and a commencement program from… Wait a minute.

I dug through the box more purposefully, finally coming up with a name on something. Sure enough, these were Abby's things.

I poked in another box; then another. None had any memorabilia from Debbie's high school career. It was almost as if she hadn't attended high school here at all.

Ruth rapped on the door, making me jump. "Are you ready yet?"

"Sorry," I said, replacing the box I was browsing in as quietly as I could. "I got sidetracked. I'll be out in a couple of minutes."

"Don't take too long," she said. "You'll make us late. I hate being late."

Chapter 8

The wine bottles clinked in the back seat as I piloted Ruth's sensible Buick to my ex-husband's house. Gene met us as I pulled into the driveway and helped his mother out of the car and up the front steps. I was grateful – not just for the help with Ruth, but also for the time to pull myself together before I went inside.

Memories crowded around me as I made my way up the sidewalk to the door: Emmy falling and skinning her knee, Tim trying to do tricks on his skateboard, all three of the kids bursting through the door at the end of the school day. I had been their favorite person back then.

Thank goodness Riley had redecorated. I might have melted in a blubbering heap, otherwise.

All our old furniture – the stuff the kids had beaten up over the years – was gone, replaced with trendy mid-century modern pieces: a low-slung sofa, Danish chairs, a kidney-shaped coffee table on spindly legs. The wall-to-wall carpet had been replaced with wood flooring and area rugs, and there was tasteful wallpaper where I'd opted for scrubbable paint in a shade that was least likely to show handprints. She'd even had the light fixtures swapped out.

"The place looks great," I told Riley sincerely when I found her in the kitchen. I presented her with the bottles of wine. "Here. Ruth says we have to drink it because she's not going to."

"She always says the same thing," she said. "I swear we're going to end up with Arnie's whole collection before it's over." Then she set down the bottles and hugged me. The gesture took me by surprise, a little, but I gamely hugged her back. "I'm *so* glad you're here," she said. "I thought you might not want to come, since, well."

"Oh, I wouldn't have missed it." I looked around. "I see you guys remodeled in here, too." Cherry cabinetry and stainless-steel appliances gleamed. "Gene must be doing pretty well for himself."

Riley shrugged. "I inherited some money from my grandparents, and I thought the place could use some freshening up. Come on – everybody's in the sunroom."

We had called it the family room when the kids were small. But larger windows had been installed, making the room lighter and airier than I remembered. Ruth was already ensconced on the settee, with two small children using her as a jungle gym.

"Careful of Nana!" Riley called. "She's still healing from her surgery."

"They're fine," Ruth said, wearing the first genuine smile I'd seen on her since I'd arrived, weeks before.

"Ryker, don't climb all over her!" said my eldest daughter from her corner.

Bea! I nearly fell over my own feet to reach her.

"Mama, who is that lady you're hugging?" the little girl on Ruth's lap called.

"She's your mama's mama," Ruth told her.

"Nooooo," the little girl said. "Bunny is mama's mama."

"Nope," Riley said. "Nana's right. I'm your step-grandma. Maggie is your *real* grandma."

I was too busy holding on to Bea and crying to see how the child – Royce, that was her name – reacted to that bit of news. And I couldn't find it in me to fault my daughter for her own daughter's misunderstanding, for Bea was crying, too.

"I'm so sorry," I said, when I could speak again. I cupped her face in both my hands.

Her expression clouded for a moment, then cleared. "I'm sorry, too." Then she pulled away from me and wiped her face with her fingers. "Kids, come say hi to your grandma."

Ruth held Ryker up to John. Royce slid from Ruth's lap as if she'd been caught doing something wrong and took her father's hand, and the three of them approached Bea and me. I knelt and held one hand out toward Royce. "How do you do?" I said.

I thought maybe Gene had taught her how to shake hands, but the confused look on her face told me I was wrong. So I raised both hands toward her, and she moved in for a hug as if she'd been doing it all her life.

As the room erupted in a chorus of *aww*s, Royce nestled in my arms and said, "My name is Royce. What's your name?"

"I have many names," I said. "What would you like to call me?"

"Gramma," she replied promptly, then frowned. "But I already have a gramma."

"She means my mom," John explained. Then he told Royce, "They can both be Grandma."

"No." She fiddled with the hem on her dress.

"What about Grammy?" Bea suggested.

"No."

"GiGi?"

"No."

"Bubbie," said Ruth.

"NO," said Royce, shaking her head.

I shot Ruth an incredulous look. "*You* should be Bubbie, not me." She sat back, speechless.

To Royce, I said, "How about Nokomtha?" That voice in my head had whispered it to me. It wasn't quite right, the voice said, but it was close enough.

Royce looked up at me in surprise and delight. "Yes! Nokomtha!"

Bea raised an eyebrow at me. God, I'd missed that look. "No-what?" she said.

I shrugged. "It popped into my head."

"What does it even *mean*, Mom?"

"It's the word for grandmother in Shawnee."

"Shawnee? Where did *that* come from?"

I had no good answer for my most practical of children, so I moved on quickly. "Here, Royce," I said, moving the little girl off my lap so I could stand. "Let me say hello to your brother." I stood and took the baby out of John's arms.

"Say hi to Nokomtha, Ryker," Royce said sweetly.

Ryker's face crumpled, and he began to howl. There was another chorus of *awws* as I handed him back to his father.

"Sorry," John said above the din.

I waved him off. "My fault. I came at him too fast."

Royce tugged on my hand. "Don't worry, Nokomtha," she said. "I'll tell him you're nice."

I smiled and pulled her toward my leg for a hug. "Thank you, dear."

Riley announced that dinner was ready, and we all filed into the kitchen. Well, most of us got in line. Royce skipped ahead; Ryker squirmed to be let down, and toddled after her. Ruth simply moved from her seat in the sunroom to one at the kitchen table. I fixed a plate for her first, then got one for myself.

Bea watched this with an odd expression on her face. "What?" I asked, amused.

"I'm just surprised to see you waiting on her, that's all. Royce, sit down and eat." She patted the chair beside her. Royce sat long enough to stuff two bites into her mouth; then she was up and pirouetting again. Ryker, on Bea's lap, was alternately picking up finger foods on her plate and arching his back. "Sit *still*," she told him.

"No," he said, and slid off her lap to the floor.

"I'll get him," John said, but Bea had already scooted her chair back to grab him. I heard a *clunk*, and Bea emerged with one hand clutching the back of her head.

A sympathetic exclamation escaped past my lips before my brain had a chance to engage.

She shot me a look of pain and embarrassment, handed the baby to John, and left the room.

"I'll get you some ice," Riley said. She grabbed a ziplock bag and some ice cubes from the freezer, and followed her.

"Nice," Gene said to me.

I stared at him. "What did *I* do?"

"She was already nervous about seeing you again, and now you've made her feel like she's Ryker's age," he said.

I looked at the other adults remaining around the table. John was steadily working his way through his meal. Ruth wore the same vacant expression she had when we had met with her surgeon that first time; in other words, she was pretending she wasn't paying attention.

"Excuse me," I said as I put down my fork, scooted back my own chair, and followed the young women's voices to what had been my daughters' bedroom. There, I knocked once and let myself in before either Riley or Bea could respond.

Bea sat cross-legged on her old twin bed and held Riley's makeshift ice bag against the back of her head. Riley perched on the edge of the bed that had been Emmy's.

I braced my back on the closed door and crossed my arms. "I figured this reunion would have its ups and downs," I said, "but I didn't think it would fall apart this soon."

"Mom," Bea groaned. "Go away."

"Nope," I said. "Move over, Riley." I sat at the foot of Emmy's old bed and gave Bea my best understanding-mom look. "You," I said, "are doing a terrific job as a parent. Your children are clearly thriving. Their behavior is age-appropriate — and completely understandable. Adult parties always disrupt kids' schedules. I remember how hard it was to settle you and Emmy down after a night at Nana and Papa's. You two would be out of sorts for days."

"Damn it," Bea said, and began to cry again.

Riley looked back and forth between the two of us. "I thought you said she was a rotten mother," she said to Bea.

"Not about stuff like this," said Bea. "That's why I could never figure it out."

"Figure what out?" I asked.

She wiped her eyes with her sleeve and glared at me. "Why it took you so long to leave Daddy," she said. "And why you left Tim with him."

"Tim was a senior," I said, eyes widening. "He wanted to stay. And the graduation requirements in Indiana might have been different – he might have had to stay in school for another... This isn't about that, though, is it?"

"This is about what you put us through," she said. "Emotionally."

I remembered belatedly that Bea was a psychologist. "I'm sorry," I said. "I'm sure it was tough for you."

"Everybody knew, Mom. All the other kids knew what Dad was doing." She glanced at Riley, who was looking at her lap. "We all saw the consequences of his actions first-hand. The girls he abused just deteriorated in front of our eyes. They would act out – they'd skip school and their grades would drop. Or they'd isolate themselves. One tried to kill herself. No, two of them did. And they all looked at us as if the whole thing was our fault."

"But you couldn't have stopped your father any more than I could have," I said.

"Except you *could* have," Riley said. "You could have done what I did: used your leaving as leverage."

"Riley's the one who made him stop, finally," Bea said.

I knew that already; Gene had as much as told me that. "It never occurred to me to try it," I admitted. "I thought if everything came out into the open, it would be worse."

"For you, yeah," Bea said. "It was already pretty awful for Tim and Emily and me. And if you'd pressured Dad, you would have saved a bunch of other girls. You never thought of them."

I shook my head. "I didn't know them. You're right. I was a monster."

Bea sighed and set the ice pack aside. "You weren't a monster. *You* were being abused, too."

"By your grandmother?"

"And by Dad. Em and I would hear the two of you fighting sometimes, Mom, even though you tried to keep your voices down. We knew he was lying when he said he'd stop, but you always believed him."

Under my blouse, the turtle throbbed with warmth. I covered it with one hand and whispered, "How many?"

Riley and Bea exchanged a look. "We figure there were about twenty altogether," Riley said. "I was one of the first. And of course he kept on after you left."

My mind reeled. *Twenty? Oh, my God...*

Bea laughed bitterly. "Tim used to say Dad's prowling was seriously affecting his ability to get a date."

"Is that why you hated me?" I asked Bea.

She sighed again. "It was just easier when you were gone. Things were so tense between you and Dad. It seemed better, that summer you were gone, because Dad wasn't dodging everybody all the time. I'm sorry I was rude to you."

I waved my hand.

"But Tim said after Em and I went away to college," Bea continued, "Dad basically was never around. His last year was awful, he said. He felt like no one was in his corner at all."

"So he left the country," I said.

"It took me a long time to put all this together," Bea said. "I was angry about everything for a really long time. I'm glad you got me counseling at the start, though. It did help, even though I thought my therapist was an idiot." She lifted a corner of her mouth. "That's what made me decide to go into psychology – I wanted to help others get better. And during my training, I had to go through counseling myself.

It's part of the requirement for the degree. That's when I really began to understand everything."

"We'll have to talk," I said. "I'm not sure I understand it all, even now." I smiled at her, and she returned it. "But you've had your degree for some time. Why have you been dodging me? I didn't get invited to your wedding; I haven't seen the kids until now…"

She looked down and shrugged. "I know. I just didn't know how to make the first move." The same corner of her mouth quirked up. "Just because I've been through analysis, it doesn't mean I'm perfect."

"I've been trying to get her to call you," Riley said. "So has John. But Bea kept saying she wasn't ready yet." She looked at Bea. "So I told her you were going to be here today, and she needed to come, too, ready or not."

"Mama!" Royce called from the other side of the door. "I have to go pee-pee!"

"I can take her," I offered.

"No, it's okay." She handed the baggie back to Riley and stood. "I'll do it. I'm the mommy."

I got up, too, and gave her a hug. "You really are doing a great job," I said.

"You're going to make me cry again," she said, hugging me back. Then she went to help Royce.

Riley and I headed back to the kitchen. In our absence, Gene had begun to clear the table. I rescued my plate and Bea's, then heated them both in the microwave. The timer went off just as Bea re-entered with Royce.

"Thanks, Mom," she said as I handed her her plate.

"Mommy! You have to call her Nokomtha!" Royce said.

"I'll explain it to her again later," Bea said out of one side of her mouth. All I could do was laugh.

Out of the blue, Ruth announced, "I'm ready to go home."

"There's dessert," Riley said. "I made your favorite – poppy seed torte."

"Cake, Nana!" Royce called out in delight. "Cake, Nokomtha!"

Ruth harrumphed and pushed her plate away. "Oh, all right. I guess it would be rude to leave before dessert."

I watched this interplay, bemused. Ruth never seemed to get under Riley's skin. I needed to ask her how she managed to stay so unruffled when Ruth tried to make it all about her. Because that's exactly what Ruth was doing right now. I was convinced she had pushed for this family get-together because she wanted to see fireworks. She wanted to watch me puddle up over the house I'd left behind, and she'd expected a shouting match between Bea and me. I hadn't been fooled by her bland expression when Gene was busy chastising me for Bea leaving the room; I was sure she was thrilled that we were making a scene. And then…nothing. Fun's over. Might as well go home.

"Can I get a glass of wine?" I asked.

"Help yourself," Riley said, and paused while cutting slices of cake to fish a corkscrew out of the drawer in front of her.

Weapon in hand, I headed to the dining room, where I'd seen a tall, thin wine rack in one corner, and began to peruse the offerings.

"That's all pretty drinkable," Gene said. I turned, startled. I hadn't heard him behind me. "But the really good stuff is behind the door there." He indicated the sideboard next to the wine rack.

"I'm happy with the cheap stuff," I said, pulling out a bottle at random. "You know me. I buy all my wine at Aldi."

He snorted, and reached past me to snag a couple of stemmed glasses from the hanging rack at the top of the tower. "I'll join you," he said. "Is that okay?"

"Suit yourself. It's your wine."

He extracted the bottle and corkscrew from my hand. "It's Dad's, to be precise. But he's in no condition to drink it these days."

"That's a popular joke around these parts. Your mother also used it," I said.

He shrugged. "Guess I need some new material." The cork came out in one piece and he poured. "*Salud,*" he said, and clinked glasses with me. The wine was red and very dry.

"So. What do you think of the place?" He gestured in an all-encompassing semicircle with his free hand.

I chose to answer the question he was really asking. "I think Riley is good for you. In a lot of ways."

"Hmm." He set his glass down on the table and supported his chin with a fist, tapping his cheek with his forefinger. "I'm trying to decide."

I quirked an eyebrow at him.

"Whether the corn-fed life has been good to you these past few years," he elaborated.

"Ah," I said. "Well, I haven't been *here*. I consider that a plus."

He smiled humorlessly. "You've gained some weight."

"Thanks for noticing."

"And you're feistier than you used to be." He picked up his glass.

"Another line you've borrowed from your mother." I was still in the corner next to the wine rack, and he was blocking my way past the table on one side. "I think your *wife* could use some help with the cake." I went the long way around the table, but he blocked my escape route again. He stood close enough that I could smell the alcohol on his breath.

"That's sexy," he said.

"What is? Backtalk?" I snorted. "You would have smacked me for it in the old days. In fact, you did. More than once."

"I never meant to hurt you, Mags," he said.

"Move, Gene," I said, and tried to sidestep him.

He slid into my path. "You know, you're still a good looking woman, even with the extra weight. But you never remarried." He leaned closer. "I wonder why?"

Involuntarily, I took a half-step back. "Not because I've been pining for you, if that's what you're thinking. Get out of my way." I stepped back the other way, and he followed me again. "I mean it, Gene!"

"I should have never let you go," he rumbled, and put an arm around my waist.

"Oh, for God's sake," I said, and pushed him away. I didn't push hard – I was using only one hand, as my wine glass was in the other one – but somehow he ended up flat against the wall. His wine flew out of his glass and splattered the wall behind him.

We stared at each other in disbelief. Then I muttered something about cleaning up the spill and hurried to the kitchen.

"What happened?" Riley asked as I snatched the paper towel holder on the counter. "I heard a thud."

Explanations would have to wait. I rushed back to the dining room, where Gene snatched the paper towels out of my hand. "You've done enough. Get lost," he growled, and ripped several off the roll to begin blotting up the mess.

I backed away and re-entered the kitchen. Everyone was staring at me – except for Ryker, who was fast asleep in Bea's arms. "Gene had a little accident with his glass," I said. "He's fine. Everything's fine." I sat down and began eating my slice of cake. It didn't go all that well with the wine.

Mouth set in a line, Riley stalked into the dining room.

I glanced around the table. Everyone's heads were ducked as they ate their cake – except Ruth. Her plate was empty and she wore a smile of contentment. She had gotten her floor show, after all.

Chapter 9

"I'm tired," Ruth said in the car on the way home. Her head was back against the neck rest and her eyes were closed. "Guess I'm not quite up to going visiting yet."

I couldn't help myself. "Oh, stop. You enjoyed yourself."

She smiled. "Those little ones take it out of you, though."

"That's not what I meant."

She cracked an eye open. "Oh?"

"Don't play coy with me." I'd kept a lid on my anger at Gene to keep from disrupting the party. But now it was blazing, and I directed it at Ruth. "You were hoping Gene would make a pass at me, weren't you?"

"Did he?" Both eyes were open now.

"You know he did. He cornered me in the dining room when I went to get the wine."

"He shouldn't have done that."

I couldn't stop to acknowledge her words. I was too busy unspooling all of my suspicions about her behavior over the past couple of weeks. "You can try to play innocent with me, but it won't work. I know how you are. You're like a spider in a web, just waiting for someone to get caught so you can watch them squirm. You expected Bea to blow up at me in front of everybody, but that didn't work. You thought the sight of my old home would bring me to my knees, but it didn't. You thought I would hate Riley, but I don't. I even told Gene she was good for him. And now you're trying to break up their marriage."

She was quiet for a few moments. "Is that what you really think of me?" she said at last.

"You were so hard on Bea," I said. "Just like you were hard on Debbie, and now Debbie won't talk to you."

"You don't know the whole story," Ruth said. "No one does."

"So what *is* the whole story?" I said. "Go on. Explain yourself."

She opened her mouth and closed it. Then she said, "Bea and I have talked it all out."

"She's your therapist?" I said. "I'm pretty sure that's against some rule."

"No, no," Ruth said. "When she was going through her program, she came and talked to me about the expectations I had for her. Or that she thought I had for her." She pursed her lips and looked out the window. We were nearly home; street lights lit some of the houses we passed and left others in darkness.

"You did expect a lot out of her. Out of each of my kids."

"I wanted what I thought was best," she said.

It was on the tip of my tongue to say that no one can know what's best for another, that we all have to make that determination on our own, that it's not fair for another adult to waltz in and made decisions on behalf of someone else. But by then, we were back at Ruth's house. As soon as I put the car in park, she had the door open and the seat belt off.

I followed her into the house and shut the front door. When I turned, she was already mounting the stairs. Clearly the conversation was done for the night.

But then she looked over her shoulder at me and said, "I just want to say one thing: I agree with you about Riley. She's been good for him in ways you can't imagine."

Try me! But I didn't say it aloud. I watched her make her way up the stairs, one slow step at a time.

I was still seething when I went to bed myself shortly thereafter. So it wasn't until the next morning that I checked my email. That's when I got the news I'd been dreading: Abby was begging off.

I am really, really sorry, but I am just not going to be able to come out and help with Ma, she wrote. *Sallie and I have contracted with a surrogate to carry a baby for us, and we've just learned that her due date has been moved up and the baby is due any day! I should have mentioned our pregnancy before, I know, and I'm sorry I didn't. But we haven't wanted to tempt fate by telling too many people. So many things could still go wrong, including the birth mother changing her mind about giving up "her" baby to a lesbian couple. But I knew you were coming up on your deadline and I just couldn't put it off any longer.*

Again, I'm really sorry. But I know you'll understand because you're a mom too.

Love, Abby

Even though I'd been expecting her to tell me she wasn't coming, I still felt like I'd been punched in the gut. I loved Abby, and I was genuinely happy for her and her wife. I couldn't think of too many other women who deserved to be a mom more than Abby did. But she was both my backstop and my leverage with the rest of the family. How was I supposed to convince anyone else to come, now that I couldn't use Abby as the model of proper behavior?

And once again, I was stuck here without an end date. When Dee gave me that two-week deadline, *or else* had hung in the air as clearly as if he'd written it on a pink slip and skewered it to my forehead with a lightning bolt. I had to be on my way home by the end of the week. I just had to.

I used Ruth's landline – the phone was so old it had a rotary dial – to call Em. "Did you know about the baby?" I asked her.

"Yeah! Isn't it great? I can't wait to have another little cousin," she said.

"I'm so glad," I said drily. "Did you know that the baby's supposed to come soon?"

"Wait, what? No. Not 'til after the holidays, I thought."

"Aunt Abby's email said the due date's been moved up."

She paused. Then she said cautiously, "Something must have happened."

I took a moment to breathe: in, out. In, out. "Em. Honey. Did Abby lie to me?"

"I'm sure she didn't, Mom." She sounded very certain. "She was all fired up to go, the last time I talked to her. She said it was high time everyone met Aunt Sallie. And she said she was especially glad you were going to be there, too, because she was dying to see you."

"I was looking forward to seeing her, too," I said, because I had been. "And meeting Sallie. You're sure she's telling the truth? She *is* an actress."

"Mom, think. You know Aunt Abby. She's not *that* good of an actress."

I grinned in spite of myself. "Yeah, I guess you're right." My smile faded. "But this really leaves me hanging out to dry, Em. Is there any chance at all that...?"

"Don't even go there," she broke in. "Finals are coming up, remember? And I've got tons of papers to grade. Not to mention my own work. I could swing it in three weeks, after the semester's over, but no way could I do it now."

"I suppose your brother's story will be the same."

"Tim's not teaching," she said, as if I was supposed to know that.

I frowned. "He told me he was teaching English in Spain."

"No," she said, with that cautious note back in her voice. "He was back in the States, I thought. In Florida."

"Florida!" I said. "How long has it been since you heard from him?"

"Maybe a week?"

"Thank you, Emily. We'll talk again soon." I hung up and dialed my son.

Of course, it went to voicemail. "Timothy Eugene Brandt," I said, in a tone I had not used with him in at least a decade, "this is your mother. Emily told me you're in Florida. I don't know what you're doing there, or why you lied to me about Spain, but you need to get your butt to Rockville immediately."

I hung up and hesitated. My next step should have been to call Gene, but after his shenanigans the night before, I wasn't in any mood to talk to him. Instead, I called Riley. I needed to touch base with her anyway.

"First," I said when she answered her phone, "I owe you an apology for last night."

"No, you don't," she said. "I got the whole story out of Gene after you left. He can be such an *asshole* sometimes." Her voice dripped with disgust.

"I think he'd been drinking," I ventured, remembering the alcoholic cloud that had seemed to envelop him when he stood close.

"He's *always* drinking," she said, and laughed. "It's like he feels like it's his job to drink all of Arnie's collection as fast as he can."

"He's an alcoholic." It wasn't a question.

"I think so, yeah."

"Well. I'm sure Ruth has already told you what to do, so I won't bother saying it." My tone came out more bitter than I'd intended.

I heard her take a deep breath. "You know," she said, "I know I said she was horrible, but she really isn't that bad. I think she's mellowed quite a bit over the past few years. You should give her more of a chance."

"I'll get right on that," I said, hoping I didn't sound too sarcastic. "In the meantime…" And I told her about Abby, and about the message I'd left for Tim. "So you and Gene may be getting a call from him soon, asking to borrow airfare," I finished.

She made an exasperated noise. "That *jerk*. I'll have Gene call him tonight."

"Thanks," I said. "Um. Did Gene tell you that I said I thought you were really good for him?"

"No, he didn't," she said, sounding pleased.

"Well, I did. And I meant it."

"Well, thanks," she said, and laughed. "But you don't need to butter me up. I'll do my best to make sure Tim does what he needs to do."

"I know you will," I said. As I hung up, I realized that of everyone in this crazy family, Riley was the only one I'd trust farther than I could throw her. Well, John, too. But what did that say about the rest of them, that the only people I trusted were the ones who had married in?

Which reminded me: I hadn't tried Debbie again. I started to dial her number, and then hung up. I could harass her from here to Sunday and she still wouldn't come home.

Nope, everything depended on my boy Tim. And he wasn't showing much of an inclination toward trustworthiness.

I'd been putting off telling Ruth about Abby backing out. I thought it would be better if I waited until I had someone lined up to come instead. Sort of a "I know your daughter's a jerk, but look, the glass is half-full anyway" ploy. But when I realized it would be Tim or nobody, I broke down and told her.

"Call Dr. Stein," Ruth said in exasperation.

"Ruth," I began.

"Not for a *date*, for God's sake," she said. "For *help*. For suggestions on what to do next. You can't possibly be the only person in his practice who has ever had this problem."

I had to admit that she was right. He had said as much to us before Ruth's surgery. "Okay, fine," I said. "But only to get his advice."

She snorted. "You're no better at asking for help than you are at taking compliments."

The turtle warmed at that, but only a little. Maybe I was getting better at this stuff. Or maybe Ruth was wrong, for once.

Still, I had to work on getting up the nerve to call – even though I was sure I'd get his receptionist. I figured I would get a call back at the end of the day, if I was lucky. But I was either really lucky or horribly unlucky, depending on how you looked at it.

"Nathan Stein."

"Oh!" I blinked a few times and pulled my thoughts together. "I didn't expect you to answer your own phone."

"Jan had to step away," he said. "Mrs. Brandt, isn't it?"

"Well, no. I mean, yes," I said, even more flustered. "But Ruth is my ex…"

"Ex-mother-in-law. I remember now." I could hear him smiling. Damn Ruth anyhow for putting absurd ideas into my head. "So what can I do for you, Ms. Brandt?"

Call me Maggie tried hard to get past my lips, but I bit it back. Instead, I gave him a brief outline of my dilemma, explained that I needed a solution immediately, and asked whether he had any suggestions.

"I may," he said. "Would you have time to stop by my office this afternoon to discuss it? Say, around five? My last patient appointment is at 4:30. That will give me time to clear out the backlog, and then we'll have time to chat."

I couldn't decide whether this was an odd suggestion or not. *Consultation first, dinner after?* Ruth was in the habit of having dinner around five; I felt a little like I was abandoning her to her own devices. But then I realized she'd been left to her own devices before I got here and had survived, more or less. Plus if she knew who I was ditching her for, she'd hold the front door open and push me toward the car.

"Uh, sure," I said at last. "That should work out fine."

I did not tell Ruth where I was going – just that I would be home late. She smiled and told me to have a good time. I suspected she already knew.

Traffic was horrible, and I was ten minutes late. Dr. Stein's office was in a mid-rise medical office building down the street from the hospital where Ruth had had her surgery. Parking in the adjoining garage was usually a miserable affair, similar to finding a spot at a shopping mall the weekend before Christmas – but now that the office staff had left, I had my pick.

His office door was locked, of course, since it was now after hours. I knocked, expecting no answer – but again, he surprised me by opening the door. "Ms. Brandt, come in," he said.

"Sorry I'm late…"

"No, no. You have perfect timing. I'd just finished my last report." He took my coat and hung it on the rack next to the door for me. "Come on back."

The last time I'd been here, we'd chatted in one of his exam rooms, with Ruth as our chaperone, kind of. Anyway, this was my first look at his office, and it was very nice – on the corner of the building, with a lovely view of the park next door. His desk was preternaturally neat, with nary a stray paper to be seen atop it – just an expanse of mahogany and a laptop computer. The office was big enough for a conversation area next to the windows: an angular sofa, a couple of chairs that looked like they were made of leather scraps and bungee cords, and a chrome-and-glass coffee table supporting an inscrutable sculpture, positioned just so. Everything was sleek and modern. I suspected he'd hired a decorator.

"Please, have a seat," he said, indicating the sofa. "Coffee? Water?"

"Water would be good, thanks," I said, and he got me a bottle from a little fridge next to the wet bar. "Nice place. You could throw a party in here."

He laughed. "You know, I'm hardly ever here. Most nights, I take my laptop home and eat in front of the TV. I'm a very boring guy."

I smiled and nodded, not knowing what to say.

"Anyway," he said. "To your problem."

"Yes." I leaned forward.

"I thought of a couple of options. One would be to hire a visiting nurse. Depending on Mrs. Brandt's insurance coverage and the level of care she would need, you could get someone to stop by once a week, once a day, or even twenty-four-hour care."

"She doesn't need that much help," I said, seeing dollar signs. "But once a day would be good."

"You could also sign her up for Meals on Wheels. That's a low-cost option, and it would give her a point of contact with another person once a day. How are her eating habits?"

"I don't know, to be honest," I said. "She eats fine when I cook, but I don't know what she does when I'm not there. I'll have to ask Riley."

"And Riley is…?"

"My ex-husband's wife."

He sat back. "Well. It's not often that you hear of a divorced woman who's so close to her ex that she feels comfortable calling the new wife."

"It's complicated," I said, hoping that would shut down further questions along those lines. "These are great suggestions. Anything else?"

He picked up a stack of brochures on the coffee table and shuffled through them. "Maybe you should check with the county department of health and human services first. They run a referral program for elder care services. And the hospital has a social worker. I'm surprised you didn't meet with her before Mrs. Brandt was discharged."

I shrugged. "Maybe she met with Ruth, and Ruth told her to take a hike."

"That sounds like the sort of thing she'd do," he said with a grin. He wasn't half bad looking, really.

But then, as he handed me the stack of brochures, I noticed his hands. I had noticed them before and thought they were appealing. But up close, I could see dark, curly hairs sprouting from his fingers. Hairy knuckles weren't a deal-killer, but they might be indicative of too much hair elsewhere. I'd never gone for the hirsute look. Gene wasn't hairless, but he didn't have back hair.

"Thanks," I said with a weak smile. "Looks like I have my work cut out for me."

"Just a couple of phone calls," he said encouragingly. "I'm sure you'll have no problem finding someone to help you."

"Well." I stuffed the brochures in my bag and rose. "I appreciate you making the time to meet with me. You could have just told me to call the social worker at the hospital."

"But then we wouldn't have had this time to chat," he said.

"True enough." I smiled more brightly.

He put a hand on my elbow. "Ms. Brandt. Maggie. Would you mind if I called you sometime?" he asked.

Hairy knuckles! But I heard myself saying, "Sure, I'd like that."

As I fled to my car, I felt the skin of my throat prickle. The turtle was as cold as ice. If that meant I'd be stepping off my mysterious path to pursue a romance with this Dr. Nathan Stein, I agreed wholeheartedly. And anyway, I didn't intend to be here long enough for him to collect.

Ruth was ecstatic to hear that Dr. Stein and I were now on a first-name basis, but she refused to look at any of the brochures he'd handed me. "No. No, no, no. I don't want anyone else in this house besides family. I don't trust them."

"Ruth, if it's a matter of money…"

"That's not the point!" she shouted. "And anyway, I'm not that sick."

"You're pretty much the definition of 'that sick,'" I said. "You just had cancer surgery."

"I'm. Fine. Dr. Stein said he got it all." She refused to look at me; she kept her eyes on the TV and clutched the remote as if she wanted to clunk me on the head with it. "I don't need anybody coming in here and poking their nose into all my business."

I threw up my hands. "So what are you gonna do when I have to go home, then?"

"You'll just have to stay." And she turned up the sound on the TV.

Chapter 10

My deadline for returning home was fast approaching, and of course my son had yet to turn up. He'd never called his father for airfare, or so Riley said, and he'd certainly never called me. I called Em again to ask her to call her brother; she didn't quite hang up on me, but she made it clear that she: a) was extremely busy; b) didn't want to be my errand girl anymore; and c) was done with this whole conversation. I promised not to bother her again until her semester was over.

That left Beatrice. I was nervous about contacting her – what if I said the wrong thing and she decided to shut me out of her life again? But in the end, I felt I had no choice.

"What I'm hearing you say," she said when I finished outlining the problem, "is that Tim has lied to you about his whereabouts, and you'd like for me to call him."

"Yes."

"And tell him what?"

"Tell him to get his butt up here!"

"You said you'd already left him a voicemail to that effect."

"Yes, and in so many words. And he hasn't responded."

I could hear her stifling laughter. "Yes, he has, Mom. You just refuse to hear it."

"Oh, really?"

"Mom," she said. "Let's play a little game. You be Tim, and I'll be you."

I rolled my eyes. "Okay. All right."

"Okay. So you're on the beach in Florida, soaking up some rays and watching the girls as they walk by in their bikinis, and your phone rings. What do you do?"

"I answer it, because it's my mother calling."

She waited.

I sighed. "Oh, all right. I look at the caller ID. It's Mom, who has called me a couple of times now about Nana."

"So what do you do?"

"I put away the phone and let it go to voicemail."

"Okay, so I'm mad that you didn't pick up, and I'm leaving you this voicemail: 'Timothy Brandt, you need to get up here and help me with your grandmother! Call me back or else!'"

I nodded, impressed. "You're good at this."

"Thanks," she said with a hint of amusement.

"Although I used his middle name, too."

She laughed. "Pulled out the big guns, did you? Okay. You're still Tim, don't forget. Are you going to listen to the voicemail?"

My eyebrows shot up. "Is there another option?"

"Sure. You could listen long enough to catch the caller's tone of voice, and then delete it. Or you could delete it without listening to it at all. Or just let it sit there and never listen to it."

"Hmm." I switched my cell phone to the other ear. "I guess it would depend on how annoyed I was with you to start with."

"Well, this isn't the first time I've called you about Nana. And I've had some family members call you, too. So you already know what's going on."

"And now you're calling to yell at me."

"Right. What would you do with that voicemail, Tim?"

"I'd spike that sucker," I said, and sighed. "But I really do need to talk to him. How can I get him to pick up the phone?"

"Let's back up," Bea said. "You're still Tim. How did you feel when you got that voicemail from me?"

I hated my answer, even though I knew it was true. "It made me feel like a kid again. You were scolding me, and that made me think about all the times you yelled at me when I was a kid. I hated that. It made me feel stupid, like I couldn't ever please you. And it also reminded me that Nana scolds me, too. And I don't want to be scolded anymore. I'm an adult now. Mom needs to treat me like an adult."

She was quiet while I let that sink in. After a few moments, she said, "So do you have any ideas for getting him to listen to you?"

I let out a breath. "It may be too late."

"Nah," she said. "This is Tim we're talking about. He'll forgive you, if you give him a chance. And anyway, it's almost never too late. *We're* talking again, aren't we?"

I smiled crookedly. "Yeah. That ought to count for something."

With the turtle warming gently under my shirt, I ended the call to Bea and called Tim again.

Of course, it went to voicemail. "Tim, it's Mom," I said. "I'm calling to apologize for my last message. I'm sorry I flew off the handle. You're an adult, and I should treat you like one. So would you please call me back so we can brainstorm solutions for Nana's situation? I need to go home at the end of this week, but I can't leave without a plan in place. Thanks. Love you. Sorry again." I ended the call and hoped I sounded contrite enough.

Half an hour later, my phone rang. "Sorry I haven't gotten back to you earlier," Tim said. "My phone got stolen and I just got this new one today."

I stifled a sigh. I wasn't sure whether to believe him, but now was not the time to challenge his story. "I understand," I said, trying to sound like I did. "I don't know whether you're up to speed on the situation…" And I spent a minute or two catching him up.

"Wow," he said. "I'm really sorry to hear all that. I wish I had the money to come up there and help out."

"Talk to your father," I said. "He'll loan you the money."

"You talked to Dad?"

"I did. But it was Riley who said you should call."

"You've met *Riley*?"

"Yeah, I have. I like her. I think she's really good for your dad." I couldn't resist adding, "Bea agrees with me."

"Whoa," he said. "You talked to *Bea*? My *sister* Bea?"

"It's been a very odd few weeks here," I said. "Nana has even been mostly tolerable."

He laughed in surprise. "I can't believe this. She must be drugging you."

"Come up and see for yourself," I said slyly.

A pause. Then, "Okay. I will."

I blinked. "Really?"

"Yeah. Let me call Dad. I've gotta see all this family togetherness in person."

He arrived the next day. Riley picked him up at BWI and brought him over. "Jesus, it's cold. I forgot what it's like here in November," he said, stooping over Ruth's recliner to give her a hug. "Hello, Nana. Hello, Mom."

I got up and hugged him fiercely. "Where's your coat?"

"I left it in Tampa. But it's okay – I've got an old one at home."

"We came straight from the airport," Riley explained.

Oh, that's right. His home is at Gene's. With Riley. I wondered how many more of these gut punches I was going to have to live through.

Tim looked good, though. Of my children, he was the one whose looks took after my family the most. Bea is all Brandt, with Ruth's slight build, and Gene's olive complexion and dark, curly hair. Emmy is only a little taller than her sister, but her hair is dishwater blond like mine. Tim is all Muir – tall and fair – although right now he was so tanned that his teeth dazzled you when he smiled. Or maybe that was just me.

"It's so good to see you," I said. "You'll have to tell me all about your travels."

"Absolutely."

"When's Debbie coming?" Ruth said.

I traded a surprised look with Riley and my son. "Did you expect her?" I asked.

"Oh, Abby," she said, chiding. "You know she always comes home for the holidays. And now that Gene's here…"

"Ruth," I said gently, "this is Tim. Gene's son. And I'm not Abby, I'm Maggie."

She looked at me sharply. Then she hoisted herself up from her chair. "I'll be right back," she said, and shuffled off in the direction of the downstairs bathroom. She was moving better every day, and she'd gotten dressed this morning in anticipation of Tim's arrival; I'd snagged her ever-present bathrobe and thrown it in the washer. But she insisted on wearing Arnie's old slippers in the house, even after I offered to buy her a new pair at Target that would fit better.

"How long has that been going on?" Tim asked, as we heard the bathroom door close. He pulled over a footstool and had a seat.

I shrugged as I settled back into my corner of the couch. "Off and on since I got here, at least."

"It's been since Papa died," Riley said. She sat at the other end of the couch. "She's much better than she was at first. But the memory problems seem to kick in when she has new people to cope with."

"That makes sense," I said, nodding. "She called me Abby once before, not long after I got here."

"Is there anything I can do to help?" he asked.

Riley and I both shook our heads. "We could mention it to John," I said, "but I don't know that there's anything that can be done at this point."

"Maybe Bea knows a social worker she could talk to," he suggested. "Sounds to me like the problem is stress."

"Do you really think Nana would go for counseling?" I said.

"Good point," Tim said with a laugh. Riley giggled, and I joined in.

"Glad everybody's in such a good mood when I'm not around," Ruth groused as she rejoined us. "Maggie, where are your manners? Why don't we have refreshments set up?"

"It's not my house," I said, but lightly. "You're the hostess here, Ruth. But I'm happy to step up. What would everyone like to drink?"

"Nothing for me, Mom, thanks." Tim pulled his footstool to the side of Ruth's recliner. "How are you doing, Nana? I heard you had to have surgery."

"I'm coping, thank you, Tim," came the prim response. And then she said, "Your mother has been a big help to me."

He shot me a surprised smile. "Yeah, Mom's pretty cool."

"I'm leaving her this house," Ruth said in a confiding tone. "Don't tell your father."

"Ruth?" I called. "Anything to drink?"

"Don't interrupt me," she said, irritated. "I'm talking with your boy here."

"Far be it from me to interrupt," I said. I caught Riley's eye and jerked my head toward the kitchen.

"Did you know about that?" Riley asked, amused. She took a seat in a dinette chair and crossed her legs twice.

I rolled my eyes. "I've been trying to talk her out of it. What am I gonna do with this house? I have no interest in moving back here."

"You could sell it," she said. "Buy yourself a house somewhere else."

"That's probably what I'd do," I said. "But I can't imagine she'll go through with it. And frankly, it worries me that she keeps going on about it." I cast a glance at the saloon doors that blocked us from the rest of the house.

"Do you think it's a symptom of whatever's going on in her brain?" Riley asked.

"No idea. I should ask John."

"Tomorrow," she said. "We're having everybody over, since Tim is here."

"Great," I said, although I wasn't crazy about seeing Gene again. "Thanks for doing the hosting duties."

She grinned. "It's no trouble. I enjoy doing it – it gives me a captive audience for trying out new recipes."

"Just another friendly service I provide. Um." I paused. "Assuming she actually did leave the house to me…is there someone in the family who would need it?"

"Someone you could give it to?" Her forehead wrinkled as she thought about it. "I mean, we have a house."

"And Abby's settled in California," I said.

Riley snorted. "If you had a choice between the weather in California and here, which would you pick?"

"A fair point," I said with a smile. "Coffee? And I think there are some cookies."

"You don't have to play hostess for my benefit," she said. "I know where everything is." She got up and got herself a glass of water.

As she filled her glass, I leaned against the counter next to the sink. "Debbie hasn't been here in thirty years. I can't imagine *she'd* want the place."

"Me neither. But maybe one of her kids…?"

"Ruth says she's written them off – that Debbie poisoned them against her." I thought back to the phone conversation. "Although I wonder how true that is, considering how many of the other things she told me that day have turned out not to be true."

"Like what?" She crossed back to her seat and took a sip of water.

"She told me you were a shrew," I said with a laugh.

She nearly did a spit take. When she could breathe again, she said, "I wonder what I did to piss her off that day."

"I don't think it was you. She also told me Abby had landed a part in a big movie." I started a cup of coffee for myself. "I think she was inventing things so I would feel like I had to come."

"I wonder why," Riley mused.

"I've been asking myself the same thing since she first called." Coffee in hand, I sat down at the dinette table across from her.

"She must feel like she has some unfinished business with you."

"If she felt the need to apologize," I said, "she could have just sent me a card."

Tim walked in just then, his smile widening when he saw us laughing together. "I've gotta say, this does my heart good," he said. He spotted the coffee machine. "Oh, cool. Got any French roast?"

"I think there's one in the sample box. See it on the counter?"

He rooted around for a moment, then held up his prize. "Score!" he said happily, and plunked it in the machine.

"So you didn't think we'd get along?" Riley said.

"Oh, no, you misunderstand," Tim said. "I always thought you two would be terrific friends, if Mom ever unbent long enough to give you a chance." He raised his cup toward me and took a seat.

"How's Nana?" I asked.

"She nodded off in mid-sentence. I'm clearly a fascinating conversationalist." He winked at us. "No, I think she's still worn out from the surgery." He sipped and made a noise of contentment. Then he focused on me. "So what's this about giving you the house? Whose bright idea is that?"

"Hers and hers alone. I'm trying to talk her out of it." I eyed him. "You don't want it, do you?"

"Hell, no. I mean, heck, no. Sorry, Mom."

I waved it away. "It's okay."

"I don't ever intend to live up here again."

"So you're going back to Europe?"

He fingered his mug and looked sideways at me. "About that."

"Yes?"

"I've actually been back for a couple of years now."

"So...no view of the Alhambra from your bedroom window, or whatever?"

"You're not making this any easier."

I lowered my hackles. "Sorry. I'm just trying to figure out why you felt the need to lie to me."

"That's what I'm trying to tell you. Just hang on a minute and let me tell it my way."

"All right. I'll shut up. You talk."

"Yeah, thanks."

"Tim," Riley said.

He looked at her and sighed. "Yeah, okay." He glanced at me and back down at his mug. "I was really mad at you when you left me with Dad."

My eyebrows shot up. "You said you wanted to stay with him."

"But you acted like you didn't want me."

"*You* acted like you didn't want *me*," I said. "And it made sense to let you stay and graduate with your friends. You would have had to change schools in your senior year, and the graduation requirements would have been different. You might have had to stay in school an extra year. And there weren't any travel soccer teams near Grandma's house. There are now, but there weren't nine years ago. I checked."

His head came up. "You did?"

"Of course I did." I squeezed his forearm. "I didn't *want* to leave you behind, Tim. I didn't want to leave *any* of you behind."

"Then why?"

"I didn't feel like I had a choice," I said. "I had to leave to save myself, and I didn't think Nana would let you guys come with me."

"She's right about that," Riley said. "You know she is. Nana wouldn't have let you go. We talked about it. And Bea told you the same thing."

He shook his head. "But you don't know what it was like, Mom. I couldn't have any friends over – I never knew what I was liable to walk in on." He cut a glance at Riley, who blushed and looked down.

"He brought them *home*?" I said, horrified. "While you were there?"

"Yeah. And I was in classes with some of the girls he was boinking, so that was awkward. And God knows I couldn't bring home anyone *I* wanted to date." He snorted. "I made that mistake exactly once. Of course, he started flirting with her. We got into a huge argument over that, and he kicked me out. I stayed with Tony and his family for a couple of weeks, until Dad said I could come home."

Tony was one of his soccer teammates, I knew. My heart hurt for my son. "Why didn't you tell me?"

"What could you have done?"

"I could have brought you to Indiana anyway," I said. "We would have worked it out. Oh, Tim. Why didn't you call?"

He shrugged. "I didn't think you wanted me."

I got up and put my arms around him, and rested my cheek on top of his head. "I did," I said. "I swear I did. I love you, Tim. You'll always be my boy."

He didn't say anything, but he slid his arms around my hips and hung on. I could feel his shoulders shaking.

Riley got up to refill her water glass. Tim stirred and loosened his hold on me. I kissed the top of his head, and he looked up at me. For a moment, I could see – in the shape of his nose, the contours of his cheeks, and the color of his lashes – the little boy he'd once been. "I'm sorry," he said, and the resemblance was complete.

"There, there," I whispered, and stroked the edge of his jaw with my thumb as I used to do. That brought me back to the present. "Ow," I said with a goofy grin.

"Sorry. I need to shave," he said.

I kissed his forehead and let him go. "Okay?"

"Yeah." He hooked a thumb inside the neck of his t-shirt and wiped his cheeks with it.

"Okay." I sat back down. "So where have you been?"

"Mexico, mostly."

"Okay. Doing what?" *Not running drugs, I hope.*

"I really was teaching English," he said, a little defensively.

"But you're not now," I said. "You're in Florida. Yes?"

"Yes." He took a swig of coffee. "See, while I was working in Mexico City, I met Ana. She was one of my students, but after the class was over for the year, we began to meet up for coffee and conversation. I was helping her with her English."

"And you fell in love with her."

His eyes lit up when he smiled.

"Did she come with you?"

"No, see, she's still in Mexico City. I had to leave because of a problem with my visa, but I'm going back as soon as it's straightened out."

"Okay. But why Florida?"

"Her brother lives there. I'm staying with him 'til I can get my visa situation worked out."

"Okay. This is going to come across as a very Mom thing to ask," I began.

"Is she interested in marrying me only to get into the United States?" he asked.

"Yeah, that was the question."

"Don't think it didn't cross my mind."

I studied him. "You don't think so."

He leaned forward earnestly. "Mom, I've met her whole family. Her parents have eight kids or something, and they're all great. And Ernesto is a legal immigrant – I've seen his green card. If Ana's scheming to get to the U.S. by marrying me, she's got a lot of people in on it with her."

"That's not impossible, but I hear you."

"And anyway, I figure we'll stay in Mexico for at least the first few years. The company I'm with is really happy with my work. I think I can get teaching jobs there indefinitely."

"But you'd be able to come home sometimes," Riley said. "Wouldn't you?"

"Of course I'd be able to come home," he said. "It's Mexico. It's not a gulag."

"What's this about a gulag?" Ruth said, pushing her way through the saloon doors. The nap must have done her good; I hadn't heard her shuffling through the dining room. And then I realized she'd put on the shoes she usually wore to the store.

"Going somewhere?" I asked her.

"I thought we needed to go to Target," she said. She eased herself into a chair at the table with a little *oof*.

"We're not going to walk out on your guests," I said.

"They're not guests," she said. "They're family."

I couldn't have agreed with her more.

Chapter 11

Later that afternoon, I went over to Riley's and spent some one-on-one time with Tim. We sat in the sunroom and went over the things he would need to know in order to help Ruth. By that point in her recovery, the list wasn't long. She was getting around okay, and was able to bathe, dress, and feed herself, so most of the duties involved cooking and cleaning. And she even did some of the cooking.

He looked over the list and said, "Tell me again why nobody wants to do this? Oh, right. Because Nana."

"That's it in a nutshell," I said.

"But she hasn't been terrible with you, has she?" he said.

"You know," I said, "this has been an enlightening trip. When your father and I got married, I was so young and so focused on myself and what I was going through. It never occurred to me then that Nana must have had reasons for behaving the way she did. Everybody just took it for granted that she was a controlling shrew and it was easier for everyone if we all just let her have her way."

"And now?" he asked.

"Well, now I can see that when she's crabby, she's covering up for something else," I said. "She snapped at me a lot when I first got here, but I could see she was scared about the cancer and having to have surgery. She just didn't want to admit it."

"That's dumb," he said. "How can people help you when you won't tell them what's really bugging you?"

"Exactly."

"So what do you suppose made her so controlling in the first place?" he asked. "Any idea?"

"Nope," I said. "But I wonder…"

He looked at me expectantly.

"Have you ever noticed how Nana keeps Aunt Debbie's room untouched?"

He nodded. "It's like a museum."

"Or a shrine." That image just kept coming back to me.

"You think she worships Aunt Debbie?" He laughed. "That's weird even for you, Mom."

"What do you mean, it's weird even for me? What else have I said that's weird?"

"Nothing you've said. But you know that little turtle thing you used to have?"

I drew it out from under my blouse. "This one?"

"Yeah, that's it. Em and I used to go into your room when we were kids and pull it out of your jewelry box and play with it."

My eyes widened, and I clutched the turtle reflexively. "You did? I had no idea."

"Don't worry," he said, raising both palms to me. "We didn't do anything bad with it. We'd just, you know, pretend it was a real turtle and move it across the floor real slow. Then we'd put it back."

I was beginning to be alarmed, given the thing's behavior over the past few weeks. "Did anything weird happen when you held it?"

"Only a couple of times," he said. "Once we got a really strong feeling that we needed to put it away, so we did. And another time it started jumping around on the floor. Em was really scared."

"Any idea when this was?" I wish I'd known. I could have correlated the turtle's behavior with what was going on at the time.

"Nope. Sorry."

"And no visions or anything?"

"Mom," he said. "What *is* that thing?"

"It's an artifact from a Hopewell Indian mound," I said.

"You mean, like a burial mound?"

And then it hit me. It likely would have come from a burial mound. And who would it have been buried with? Me. Or the me I was when I was a Hopewell. After I'd received the turtle in that ceremony in the Great Circle.

"Mom?"

I'd been buried in a mound in Indiana, and that idiot of a farmer had desecrated my tomb because it was in the way of his plow. Oh, there would be hell to pay when I found him...

"Mom!" Tim touched my wrist, and I jumped. He pointed at the hand that still held the turtle. "You turned it on somehow."

I looked down. He was right. Not only was my hand warming rapidly, but the turtle itself was glowing with a pulsing yellow light.

Breathing hard, I pulled the chain over my head and threw it on the floor, whereupon the light immediately went out.

Tim crouched to look at it. "Don't touch it," I said.

He glanced up at me, startled. "I won't. Don't worry. But..." He examined it carefully. "It looks cleaner than I remember it. Have you been polishing it?"

"No. The tarnish is burning off by itself." I weighed my next words. Tim was not my most accepting child when it came to the supernatural – that would probably be Emmy – but I had been bursting to talk to somebody about this stuff for a couple of weeks, and he was the only one handy. "Look, this is going to sound odd. But that thing" – I crouched next to him and pointed to it – "I believe it was mine in a past life." And then I told him about my vision in the Great Circle, and about meeting Granny and Zed in the parking lot. Not all of the details, but enough so he got the gist of it.

He dropped to a seat on the floor. "Wow. That's weirder than I would have pegged you for."

I stood and took a seat on the settee. "You think I'm crazy."

"Not necessarily. I've been living in Mexico, remember? The weekend before I left for Florida, Ana and I spent a day at the Teotihuacán Pyramids. When did the Hopewell live, anyway?"

"From about 100 to 500 A.D.," I said.

He nodded. "That's what I thought. They were roughly contemporaneous with the culture that built Teotihuacán. And the structure of the pyramids is reminiscent of the Cahokian culture in the Mississippi valley later on." He laughed at the expression on my face. "Don't look at me like that. Just because I was a jock, it doesn't mean I wasn't interested in other stuff."

"I never said it did." I'd always thought that if Tim had been left to his own devices, he might have become the anthropologist I'd never had the chance to become. "It was Nana who pushed you into sports."

"True." He shrugged. "Anyway, we climbed the Pyramid of the Sun. It's a *lot* of steps, and I'm not in the same kind of shape I was in high school. But as we climbed, I could feel something happening to me. Something loosened inside me." He shook his head. "I know it sounds crazy. But I mentioned it to Ana, and she said she felt it, too. So we sat up there for a little while, and then we went down the avenue and climbed the Pyramid of the Moon. And *that* was like…" He paused. "I don't even know how to describe it, other than to say that whatever had loosened up inside me at the Sun pyramid was moved into a different alignment at the Moon pyramid." He gazed at me steadily, earnestly. "I don't think I could have made the trip up here today without having had that experience first. A lot of things have been falling into place for me since we made that visit."

"I wish I could say the same thing about my life since my experience in the Great Circle," I said with a laugh. "It seems like everything that's happened since then has just made me more confused."

"It'll sort itself out," he said. Then he gestured toward my necklace, still on the floor where it had landed. "You must be making some kind of progress, Mom. The turtle is cleaning himself up."

"Herself," I said, surprised.

He watched me, smiling. "You just now figured that out, didn't you?"

"I just now *remembered* it," I said.

His grin widened. "See? It'll all work out. It just has to be the right time. Or maybe right now, you're loosening everything up, and the alignment will come later."

I picked up the necklace and slid it over my head. "I guess we'll find out, one way or another."

Ruth had a checkup scheduled with her regular doctor – Bea's husband – the next morning. As I drove her to the appointment, she said, "You know, I knew John before he married Bea."

"Did you."

"Yes. In fact, I was the one who introduced them." She nodded self-importantly.

I made a note to check the claim with Bea later, and pulled up my mental list of things to ask John about at this visit. Ruth's episodes of confusion were high on the list.

When the nurse called Ruth's name, she clutched my sleeve. "Come with me," she said.

"Why?"

"Just do it," she hissed.

So I got up and went with her to the door where the nurse stood. "I see you brought a helper today, Mrs. Brandt," she said loudly, with a bright smile.

"Is it okay for me to go back with her?" I asked.

"Sure, if it's okay with the patient," the nurse said. "Is it okay with you, Mrs. Brandt?"

"Yes," said Ruth tiredly. "It was my idea in the first place. And please don't treat me like a child."

The nurse's expression hardened. "This way," she said, and whirled.

"Don't be a jerk to the nurse," I whispered.

"Well, she ought not to patronize me," she said in a normal tone. "'I see you brought a helper today.' Like I'm a three-year-old." She raised her voice. "And I'm not deaf, either."

The nurse, to her credit, was personable and professional as she checked Ruth's vital signs and asked her the usual questions. But I was sure we would be a topic of conversation in the nurses' lounge later in the day.

"Dr. Simms will be with you in a few minutes," she said at last, and walked out. She might have closed the door a little more firmly than was necessary, but maybe I was just sensitive, given Ruth's shenanigans.

Ruth was eyeing me from her perch on the exam table. "Just wait 'til you get to be my age," she said. "We'll see how you react when some young nurse treats you like a toddler. I wish I could be there to see it."

"You'll outlive us all," I said.

"Hmph. Not likely." She stared out the window and said nothing more.

I added *Comments about imminent death* to my list of stuff to ask John about.

A few minutes later, John knocked and let himself in. "Whoa, nobody told me there was a party in here," he said.

"Where?" said Ruth.

"Nice to see you, Maggie." He shook my hand. "Ruth, always a pleasure. I see you're still refusing to wear our fashionable gowns."

"I won't be caught dead in one of those paper monstrosities. You know that."

"I do, because you tell me every time you're here."

And so on. At one point, I broke in and said, "Can I get a copy of the script?"

John laughed. "We understand one another, that's all."

"Yes," said Ruth. "I understand you're trying to kill me."

John laughed, but Ruth didn't look like she was joking.

At the end of the exam, John sat on his spinning stool and said, "Looks to me like you're as healthy as ever, my dear, although I'm a little concerned about that incision in your navel. When do you see Nathan again?"

"Tomorrow," I responded.

He looked at both of us in turn. "Have him take a look at it."

"Okay," said Ruth. "Can I go now?"

"I've got a couple of questions, John, if you've got another minute," I said.

Ruth looked disgruntled. "Do you need me for this? My back hurts. I need a more supportive seat than your exam table."

"I know, I know," said John, giving her a hand off the table. "Why don't you go out to the waiting room? And Maggie, come on back to my office, so the nurse can prep the room for the next patient."

"Do you know the way to the waiting room, Ruth?" I asked sweetly.

"Go soak your head," she grumbled.

I followed John out of the exam room. "I'll take that as a yes," I told him cheerfully.

He grinned over his shoulder. "This way."

His office was small and cramped, with medical books, printouts, and forms piled haphazardly on his desk. I couldn't help but contrast it with Nathan Stein's office. You could tell John actually used his – and he didn't make nearly as much money as the surgeon. "Have a seat, if you can find one," he said, shutting the door.

I squeezed into a guest chair while he took a seat behind his desk. "Now then," he said when he'd moved a stack of files that had blocked his view of me, "what've you got?"

First, I outlined Ruth's memory lapses. "Twice now, she's thought I was Abby," I said. "The memory problems seem to happen when she's under some sort of stress. It was worse when I first arrived. And then when Tim got here yesterday, she slipped again."

"Well," he said, "stress can cause havoc with anyone, as I'm sure you know. I haven't seen any evidence personally that she's developing dementia – but as you say, we have sort of a script when she comes in for an exam, and she may just be telling me what she thinks I want to know."

"Which brings me to my other concern," I said. "She's told me a couple of times now that she doesn't believe she'll live much longer. Is that true? Or is she just after sympathy?"

He leaned back and steepled his fingers, then sat forward again because another stack of papers was blocking his view from that position. "I should clean this place up," he said.

"In all your free time," I said. "Don't worry about it."

"Thanks. But to your question," he said. "The uterine cancer was the immediate concern. But Ruth has had a heart condition for a number of years."

"Oh?"

"Oh, yes. In fact, she suffered a silent heart attack about six months before Arnie's death. She's on medication for it – a blood thinner, a cholesterol pill, and a baby aspirin, once a day. Have you seen her taking them?"

"No. This is all news to me."

"Hmm. Nathan may have told her to stop prior to her surgery. But she should be starting them back up, now that she's recovering." He tapped his forefingers against his chin. "Let me give Nathan a call. I want to give him a heads up about that incision of hers anyway. And check around the house to see if you spot any pill bottles. She may have hidden them in her room when she knew you were coming."

"Okay."

"I'll ask her about them at Gene's tonight, too. No need to bring it up to her now. I know she's itching to get home."

I smiled weakly. "I'll try to scout around this afternoon, and let you know tonight what I've found. If anything."

"Thanks. I'm concerned now that she ran out of the blood thinner and just quit taking it. I know Arnie's death really hit her hard. She may have decided it's not worth going on, especially after the cancer diagnosis." He put one hand to his chin as he thought for a moment. Then he dropped it. "Well, let me give Nathan a call. Thanks for bringing this up, Maggie."

"Sure," I said. "See you tonight."

Ruth gave me a gimlet eye when I emerged from the back, but she didn't say anything until we were in the car. "What did you two talk about without me?" she demanded.

"The weather," I shot back.

"You told him I called you Abby, didn't you?"

"I might have."

"That was an honest mistake, Maggie. I was always calling my kids by the wrong name. Ask Gene."

"Did you ever think he was Abby?" I asked.

She looked studiously out the window.

"Why didn't you tell me you had a heart condition?"

"It's not any of your business," she said, still not looking at me.

"It is if I'm here supposedly helping you get better."

"From cancer," she said. "The heart problem isn't going to go away ever." Then she muttered, "Until I die."

"Are you taking the medicines John prescribed for you?"

She looked at me at last. "Why?" she asked suspiciously.

"I'm just asking," I said. "He told me you're supposed to be taking three pills every day. I've never seen you take so much as a Tylenol for a headache."

"I don't get headaches," she said.

"You're missing the point," I said.

"No, I'm not. I got your point. I just don't think it's any business of yours whether I take those heart pills."

"You *want* to die?" I said, hating myself for saying it. Melodrama was Ruth's turf, not mine. "Then why have the surgery at all?"

"Because cancer is a horrible way to go!" she cried. "Think about it, Maggie. Would you rather have a slow, lingering, painful death, or simply go to sleep and never wake up?"

"I dunno, Ruth. Seems to me you're dead either way. I'd rather live as long as I can." We were stopped at a light. "Want to go out for lunch?"

"No. I need to go home and take my pills," she said, her words heavily laced with sarcasm. "And then I'm calling my lawyer."

"You're giving the house to someone else?" I said. "Good."

"No, I still need to sign the papers," she said. "I'd been wavering. But after this conversation?" She laughed shortly. "You're definitely getting the house."

Chapter 12

Ruth fell asleep in front of the TV after lunch. As soon as I heard her snoring, I crept up the stairs. The door to her room was shut, so I eased it open and slipped inside, then shut it behind me.

I felt like a sneak thief. But if she woke up, came upstairs, and caught me, I figured I could blame my snooping on John.

The master bedroom had a bathroom attached. I checked the vanity in there first, thinking she might keep the pill bottles next to the sink. Nothing. No prescription bottles in the medicine cabinet, either, except for an extremely out-of-date one with Arnie's name on the label. I made a note of the name – Elavil – and put it back where I found it. The name faintly rang a bell; I assumed I'd heard it on a TV commercial, but I couldn't remember what the drug was supposed to do. I planned to look it up later.

On to the bedroom. It was obvious which side of the bed was Ruth's – the nightstand was overrun with magazines, tissues, and a glasses case, among other things. I spotted one prescription bottle, but it was for the pain medication Dr. Stein had prescribed for her after her surgery. I had picked it up at CVS myself. I opened the container and counted the remaining pills; it looked like she had stopped taking them after the first couple of days home. She'd told me at the time that she didn't like how loopy they made her feel.

I opened the nightstand drawer; it was full of pens, scraps of paper, and other oddments. Most of the notes were in Ruth's handwriting, but some were in block letters, childishly done, proclaiming her to be the "Worlds Best Mom!" I smiled, thinking of a similar stash of my own at home.

At the very bottom of the drawer was a plastic hospital ID band. Someone had written on it in ballpoint:

Brandt
6/17/68, 5:27 A.M.
Sex: M
6 lbs. 4 oz.

I took a photo of the band with my phone and hid it under everything in the drawer again. I made a cursory inspection of the top of both dressers and rifled quickly through their top drawers. I saw no pill bottles anywhere other than the places where I'd already spotted them. That was curious enough – but my mind was now busy on a different question: whose baby bracelet was Ruth keeping in the top drawer of her nightstand?

I sneaked back out into the hallway and paused. Ruth was still snoring. I closed her bedroom door softly, went down the hall to Debbie's room, and locked that door behind me. Then I began to tear the place apart.

Gene, I knew, was born in the mid 1950s, three years before me, so it couldn't possibly be his. Debbie's kids wouldn't have had Brandt on the wristband; she'd taken her husband's last name, which was Schmidt, and all four of their kids were Schmidts, too. And anyway, the timing was wrong. Her eldest child was only a few years older than Bea, who was born in '84.

I supposed it would have been possible for Ruth to have had a late-in-life baby. Abby would have been about eight when Baby M was born; that's a big gap, but I'd heard of bigger.

But if Ruth had had a fourth child, what had happened to him? Did he die in infancy?

I had trouble believing Ruth would have kept her mouth shut about losing a second son. No, my gut told me somebody else was Baby M's mother.

And I just kept thinking there was a reason Ruth hadn't redecorated this room at any point over the past thirty years.

I came to the box of Abby's high school stuff – and now that I was on the alert for discrepancies, I realized I'd seen one earlier but hadn't made the connection. Abby's prom invitation was orange-and-black, her high school's colors. But Debbie, who presumably would have gone to the same high school, had hung blue-and-white pompons on the wall.

I put the box of Abby's stuff back, and stood in the middle of the room, one finger on my chin, while I thought. If I wanted to put away something that I didn't want anyone to find easily, where would I put it? There was nothing under the bed – I'd already looked. The closet, maybe?

I checked. And there, behind a rack full of adorable shoes with one-inch heels, I found it: a shoebox with the name "Lenny" written on the top. Inside was a lock of dark hair tied with blue thread; a pair of baby shoes; a Baltimore Orioles baby t-shirt with snaps in the crotch, the price tag still on it; and a birth certificate from the State of Louisiana, Orleans Parish, for Leonard Eugene Brandt, born June 17, 1968 to Deborah Leah Brandt and Father Unknown.

I looked again at the baby's name, and was about ninety-five percent sure that I knew who the father was.

A little more digging, and I was satisfied. All the high school memorabilia was Abby's; Ruth and Arnie must have boxed it up and moved it in here when they remodeled Abby's room. None of it was Debbie's because, I was certain, Debbie hadn't gone to high school in Maryland at all. As soon as she found out she was pregnant, her parents probably shipped her off to a distant relative or a home for unwed mothers. The plan might well have been for Debbie to move home after the baby's birth and have Ruth and Arnie raise the child as their own while Debbie resumed her academic career. But for whatever reason, Debbie had not come home. She'd stayed in New Orleans instead. Finished high school, gone to college, married a doctor, had four kids.

No – had four *more* kids. None of whom was named Lenny.

My cell phone rang, startling me so that I overturned the box of baby things on my lap. I fumbled my phone from my jeans pocket with one hand as I tried to shove stuff back in the box with the other. "Hello?"

"Hi, Maggie, it's Riley. How did the doctor visit go this morning?"

It felt like that visit had been days ago. "Fine. She and John are regular comedians together."

"I'm not surprised. Say, would you mind stopping at Penzey's on your way over? I thought I still had some cinnamon sticks, but I guess I used them up the last time I made this recipe."

"Sure. Oh!" I glanced at the clock in sudden panic. "What time is it?"

"It's not even three yet. Are you okay? You sound rattled."

I looked down at the jumble in my lap and laughed nervously. "Rattled is a pretty good word for it. I think I've found the skeleton in the Brandt family closet."

"Ooh. Do tell."

"Tonight," I promised. "I need to make a phone call first."

"Now I can't wait," she said. "Don't forget the cinnamon sticks, okay? Get the Indonesian ones."

"Sure, no problem. I'll remember." We said goodbye and ended the call. Then I called Debbie. I was prepared to leave a message, but she surprised me by picking up.

"It's Maggie," I said. "How are you doing?"

"Fine. Listen, I'd dearly love to chat, but I need to run out and…"

"Tell me about Lenny," I said.

I wasn't sure what her reaction would be. I figured either she would say she had no idea who Lenny is and was this some kind of a joke, or she'd just hang up in my ear. But maybe some of Tim's mojo from his hike up the pyramids was working on his aunt – or maybe my turtle, which warmed as I clutched it, was involved. Because after what seemed like an eternity, she sighed and said, "How did you find out?"

"A lot of guesswork," I admitted. "John asked me to look for prescriptions in your mother's room. She had a heart attack before she was diagnosed with cancer – did you know that?"

"No," she said. "Abby never told me."

"Abby may not have known. Ruth didn't bother telling *me*, and I'm supposed to be here helping her get better." I shook my head. "Anyway, when I was snooping through her nightstand, looking for pill bottles, I found a hospital wristband with a date that didn't match anybody's birthday I knew. So I've been digging around in your old room, and found a shoebox with his birth certificate in it."

"It's a duplicate," she said. "I gave it to Daddy for safekeeping. He was supposed to put it with ours – mine and Gene's and Abby's."

"Gene is Lenny's father, isn't he?" I asked.

Silence. Then she said, "We used to play around, from the time we were little. You know how kids do – you show me yours and I'll show you mine, right? We had no idea what we were doing. It's not like kids got sex education back then, the way they do now." She sounded defensive.

"I'm not judging you," I said quietly.

"I didn't say you were," she said, with a touch of her usual asperity. Then she backed off. "Anyway, as we got older, I guess we kind of realized we weren't supposed to be fooling around with each other that way. No one was more surprised than the two of us when he came the first time." She paused. "Well, anyway. It got to be an obsession for him, and we started to get careless. Abby caught us at it one day when we forgot to lock the door, and she told on us. But by then I was pregnant anyway." She sucked in a ragged breath.

"How old were you?" I asked, even though I'd already done the math.

"Fifteen. Old enough to know better, Ma said."

"And Gene was just thirteen."

"Yeah." She sniffed.

"So what happened?"

"Well, I couldn't stay at home. Now girls flaunt their baby-mama status at school right up to delivery, but it just wasn't done back then."

"I remember," I said.

"Ma found out about a boarding school here in New Orleans where I could keep up my schoolwork while I waited for the baby to come. Then the school arranged for him to be adopted."

"Was he...normal?" I had visions of birth defects, hemophilia – all the genetic issues that could happen to a child whose parents are siblings.

"Oh, yeah. He was beautiful." She began to sob. "I'm sorry," she managed to say.

"Don't apologize. You were in an awful situation." I let her cry for a few minutes, and then I said, "You were supposed to move back home after the baby came, weren't you?"

She sighed. "You know what it's like when you get away from someone who's been oppressing you for a long time? I know you do."

"You're right," I said, thinking of my escape to Indiana. "I do."

"Well, it was like that for me, too, except I didn't realize I'd been oppressed until I got away. Ma had controlled me my whole life. And you know, when I say that to friends here, they say, 'Oh, it couldn't have been that bad. Every parent does that. That's how they raise you right.' And I keep saying, not like this. Not like this at all."

"I hear you," I said. "So you refused to come home."

"Yeah, and Ma was fit to be tied. But there wasn't anything she could do about it. I'd confided in one of my teachers at the school, and she believed me. She and her husband took me in as their ward until I turned eighteen." She blew her nose. "I thank God for Mr. and Mrs. Chalmers every day of my life."

"Ruth didn't try to get you back?"

"Sure she did. A number of times. But Mr. Chalmers finally said that if she ever tried it again, he'd have the authorities take Gene and Abby away, too." She was quiet for a moment. "I'm not sure she'd let me come home, at this point. I've been away so long, and you know how she is."

"Are you kidding? Of course she'd let you in. She keeps your room just as it was when you left – pompons on the walls and everything."

"Oh God," she said. "Would you please throw those things out? They're from when I was a cheerleader in junior high."

"Maybe you should come home and do it yourself," I said. "I don't think Ruth will let me touch them. She gave me a hard time for using a blank piece of paper from your desk."

She sighed again. "I suppose at some point, I'll have to come back and have it out with her. I do think about it sometimes, but then..." She blew her nose again.

"Maybe this will help," I said. And then I gave her my insight – that Ruth was at her most difficult when she was scared or anxious. "I expect she spent a lot of time being anxious about the three of you," I said. "The '60s were a crazy time – the drugs and the loud music and the free sex..."

"And there we were, doing it right under her nose," she said. "I know you're right. I can see that now, having raised four kids." She paused. "I just need more time."

"I'm not pushing you," I said. "But I don't think she's taking her heart medicine the way she's supposed to. If she goes, it may be quick – and you will have lost your chance."

"No time like the present, huh?" she said. "Thanks, Maggie. I'll think hard about what you've said."

"One more thing," I said. "Have you ever tried to find Lenny? He must be in his forties by now."

"I did try, some years back, but it was a closed adoption. I couldn't get any information on where he'd been placed or anything. I think the law has changed since then, though. Maybe I should try again."

"I think you should," I said. "It's clearly still bothering you. And what a gift to give Ruth, if you came home to her with news of her oldest grandchild."

"She might even let me in the door," Debbie said with a small laugh. "Maggie, thanks again. I'm glad you called today."

"So am I," I said, and ended the call. Then I put everything back in the box, and loaded it into a tote bag to take to Riley's that night. Bea and Tim deserved to know they had a brother, and I was tired of secrets.

Chapter 13

Ruth didn't notice the tote bag until we got out of the car. "What's that?" she asked, as I fetched it and the Penzey's bag from the trunk.

"Something I want to show my kids," I said, and led the way in.

Ruth made a beeline for her favorite seat on the sunroom settee. I handed the Penzey's bag to Riley and said, "How's it going? Is everyone here?"

"Yup. You're the last. Thanks." She dropped two of the sticks into a slow cooker on the counter next to the stove.

"What are you making?" I asked, looking over the array of spices on the counter.

"Moroccan chicken," she said, adding things to the pot. "The kids love it. And it makes the house smell amazing." She flashed me a grin.

"When you get to a good stopping place, come on out to the sunroom. I've got something to show everyone." I held up the tote bag.

"Ooh," she said. "I love a mystery. I'll be out in a minute. Want something to drink?"

"I'll get it," I said, and pulled one of my old glasses out of the cabinet. "Hey, you kept these."

"I like them," she said with a smile.

I gave her a one-armed hug and filled the glass at the sink. No wine for me tonight – I'd need a clear head for this, and I wasn't interested in giving Gene another opportunity to corner me.

Although with the way he glowered at me when I entered the sunroom, I was pretty sure he had no intention of trying anything. I nodded pleasantly to him. *If you think you're mad at me now, buddy, just wait.*

Ryker and Royce had already claimed Ruth's lap, but they both ran to me when they saw me. I set down the tote bag and took a minute to greet them properly, and then hugged Bea and Tim, who had been in conversation when I entered – Bea in a wicker armchair and Tim on the matching padded stool.

"What's this?" Royce asked, trying to unzip the top of the tote bag.

"It's for later," I said.

"Leave it alone, Royce," Bea said.

Of course, Royce ignored her. "Is it a present?" my granddaughter wanted to know, as I stowed it back on my shoulder.

"Nope."

"What is it?"

"Royce, come here and sit with Uncle Tim and me," Bea commanded. Royce, pouting, complied at last.

John moved in to scoop up Ryker and greet me. "Did you have a chance to...?" he asked quietly.

"Yes," I said. "And no, I didn't find anything. Sorry."

He shot an annoyed look at Ruth. "She's been telling me for the past year that she's taking them. I wonder now whether she ever filled the prescriptions at all." He looked back at me. "I'll have a talk with her."

"Good luck," I said.

"I may need it. Thanks for snooping." He gave me crooked smile.

"Thank *you* for giving me a reason to snoop. I found answers to a few of my own questions." I patted the tote bag. "I might have a bright future ahead of me as a private eye."

He laughed. "Glad to assist."

My turtle, under my blouse, warmed to a comfortable temperature. I decided it was a good omen for what was to come.

Riley poked her head in the door. "Dinner should be ready in about forty-five minutes. Anyone need a refill? Gene?"

"I'm good," he said from his corner. He seemed to have retreated into the shadows, although my impression might have been colored by what I'd learned that afternoon.

Ruth asked for water, and Riley got her a glass. Then she settled on the other end of the settee, as John pulled up a chair next to Ruth. "Maggie has show-and-tell for us," Riley said with a mischievous look.

"I have something to show, anyway," I said. "I hope others will help me with the telling." And I unzipped the tote bag and drew out the box.

As soon as Ruth saw it, she looked at me with murder in her eyes. "Give me that," she said.

"No."

"You had no right to bring that here!" she cried. "You have no right to go poking into other people's business, Abby!"

Bea and Riley sat back in surprise. John looked at his son and said, "Come on, buddy. Let's go see what's new in the playroom."

"Take Royce," Bea said.

"No! I wanna see the box!"

"Mommy will tell us all about it later," he said, and scooped her up, too. He and Bea shared a kiss, and then he took their squirming kids away.

"Who's Lenny?" Tim asked, when the little ones were out of earshot.

"Your half-brother."

"What?" That was Bea.

"Goddamnit, Maggie!" Gene stormed out of his corner and tried to rip the box out of my hands. "You're a grade-A bitch, you know that? What gives you the right?"

I shoved the box behind me on the chair. "What gave *you* the right to hide this from our children for all these years? They deserve to know they have another sibling, don't you think?"

"I don't know what game you're playing," he growled. "But you should at least have some respect for Ma. She's old and sick. You know that."

Ruth let out a sob, and covered her face with her hands.

Gene took the opportunity to grab again for the shoebox, but I held on. In the struggle, the lid fell off, and the contents fell to the floor.

Both of my kids were on their feet. "Dad! Stop!" Bea cried, as Tim stepped between his father and me. Gene stood there, fists clenched and chest heaving.

"For God's sake, Gene," Riley said, with an arm around Ruth. "What's this all about?"

"Tell her," Gene said to me, shaking a finger at his wife. "Now that you've brought it up, let's air *all* the dirty laundry."

I kept my eyes on him as I bent to pick up the mangled box. I placed everything inside except the birth certificate, which I handed to Bea. Tim put an arm around her shoulders and they studied it together.

"Leonard Eugene Brandt," she read aloud, and both of them looked at me.

"Born in 1968 in New Orleans," I said. "Aunt Debbie is his mother, and his father is…" I nodded toward Gene.

"I'm a rotten mother," Ruth keened.

"Why did she call you Abby?" Bea asked.

"Abby's nothing but trouble," Gene spat. "She caught us at it and told Mom."

"You had sex with Aunt Debbie?" Tim said. "Dad, how could you?"

"We were experimenting," he said. "It was just that one time…"

"That's not what Debbie told me," I broke in. "She said you two went at it for years."

He sat down heavily next to Riley, who scooted a little away from him. "We were just kids," he said. "Just playing around."

I shook my head and turned to my kids. "Debbie was sent to a boarding school for unwed mothers in New Orleans. After she had the baby, she refused to come home." I looked at Ruth, whose sobs had subsided. "She said she didn't realize how oppressive it had been at home until she got away."

"Someone kill me," Ruth moaned. "I've ruined everything."

"You haven't ruined anything, Ma," Gene said soothingly. Then he turned to me. "It's Maggie who's responsible for this."

"You can't really believe that," Bea said, eyes wide.

"She's caused nothing but trouble since the day I met her," he said. "Saddled me with you three brats. And then she got old and saggy – and got all weepy when I went out and looked for something better. She was always after me to give up the internship program, but I wasn't about to give *that* up, no sir. I was *glad* when she left me – did you know that, Maggie? It meant I didn't have to put up with your disapproval anymore." He turned a grateful smile on his mother. "Ma loved me anyway. She didn't care."

"*I* cared," said Tim.

"What the hell are you talking about?" said Gene.

"When I was still in high school, after Mom left, and you were bringing home girls from my class to have sex with?" Tim said, teeth bared. "I cared about that, Dad. I cared a *lot*. It made me sick to my stomach, if you want to know the truth."

"That's crap," Gene said. "You never said anything about it."

"How was I supposed to tell you? I was just a kid!"

"Why didn't you go live with your mother, then?" Gene sneered. "Oh, that's right. She *abandoned* you."

"And who told him that?" I put in. "You did. Every chance you got. You and Ruth made sure he believed he had no way out."

"I just wanted my family around me," she said, eyes closed. The tears had stopped.

I gentled my tone. "That's why you insisted that I move here when I got pregnant, isn't it? Because you'd lost your first grandchild."

"And my daughter!" she cried. "I needed to keep you close. I needed to keep *all* of you close." She looked hard at Gene. "But it didn't work. You were the only one who stayed, and only because I was protecting you." She spat her last words.

"Dad, you need counseling," said Bea. She looked at me. "I can't believe none of this came out sooner. Why didn't any of the parents press charges?"

"That, I don't know," I said.

But Ruth did. "Papa paid them off."

"What?" Gene said.

She gave him a sad smile. "You didn't really believe you were invincible, did you? Of course he paid them off. The parents didn't mess with *you*. They knew where the real money was. So they would threaten to come after the business." She shrugged. "We would have lost everything if any of the cases had gone to court, so Arnie paid them off. Worked every time. Except for the last one." Her face crumpled. "That guy wouldn't go away. Kept asking for more and more money. It was just so stressful for your father."

"So he killed himself," I said. "It wasn't due to a money-laundering investigation at all."

"Oh, my God, no," Ruth said, stricken. "Is *that* what people are saying? No, Arnie was an honest businessman. And a good man! He loved his family. He would have done anything for us."

Up to, and including, cover for his son, the pedophile.

"I didn't know," Gene said.

The kitchen timer dinged. Riley, head held high, scooted past Gene without touching him.

"Does Em know?" Tim asked, as Riley banged around in the kitchen.

I shook my head. "I haven't had a chance to call her yet. Someone should call Abby, too." I turned to Ruth. "Debbie asked me to throw away those pompons on the wall in her room. I told her to come home and do it herself."

"Will she?" she asked.

"I don't know. I think she's thought for a long time that she wouldn't be welcome."

"That's crazy!" Ruth said. "Of course she's welcome. She should come for Hanukkah next month. I'll get out the old menorah – the one we used when she was little."

"Her children may not come," I reminded her. "They're not little anymore."

She sighed and nodded. "I guess not. I've missed so much."

I thought about telling her that Debbie would look for Lenny, but I decided against it. There was no guarantee she'd find him, and I didn't want to get her hopes up.

Tim started, and reached into his pocket for his phone. "Hello? Ernesto! *¿Qué tal?... Bien, bien. Estoy con mi familia para la cena... ¿Cómo?*" The color drained from his face. "*¡Ay, no! ¿Cuándo?... Sí, sí, por supuesto. Estaré allá mañana... No, no, está bien, muchacho. Mi mamá entenderá... Hasta luego.*"

"What is it?" I asked as he stowed his phone.

"It's Ana. There's been an *accidente.* Sorry – an accident. At her job. She's in the hospital in Mexico City."

"Go," I said.

His eyes were wild. "Are you sure? But what about *your* job?"

"Maybe I was never meant to keep it," I said. "If they don't understand there are more important things in life than earning money, I don't want to work there anyway." I heard a door *snick* shut, and looked around for it, puzzled. The sound didn't correspond to any of the doors I was familiar with in this house.

"Where's Dad?" Bea asked. His seat on the settee was empty.

"Gone," Ruth crooned. "All my children are gone. They've all abandoned me because I'm such a terrible mother. I wish I could die."

"Who said that?" I said sharply.

Ruth looked at me, startled.

"Who said you were a terrible mother? Who told you that?"

"Bubbie. Bubbie did."

"Your grandmother told you you were a terrible mother," I said. "And you believed her."

"It was true!" she cried.

"Why did she call you a terrible mother?"

"Because I wouldn't spank my children when they misbehaved," she said.

"But Nana," Bea said, "you were right. You *shouldn't* spank your children."

Ruth looked at Bea, surprised. "You shouldn't?"

"No," she said. "It doesn't help the child learn anything except how to avoid being spanked."

"I was right?" she said.

"Yes, Nana. You were right."

Ruth looked off into space. "All these years," she said. "All these years."

Riley came to the doorway. "I don't know if anyone has any appetite left, but dinner's ready."

"Where's Gene?" I asked her when I passed.

Her mouth twisted. "I don't know, and I don't care. He tried to cuddle up to me while I was cooking. I told him to get away from me. So he took his car keys and left." She shook her head. "If I'd known about all this a few years ago…"

"Believe me," I said. "If I'd known, I wouldn't have married him, either."

Dinner, and the children's antics, revived us – except Tim, who gobbled his meal, and excused himself as soon as he was done.

Bea took John aside and gave him the short version. When he returned to the table, he extracted a promise from Ruth that she'd begin taking what he had prescribed for her. He told her it was the only way to ensure she'd live long enough to see Debbie come home. When he put it to her that way, she eagerly agreed, and even told me to make sure we stopped to pick up the pills on our way home.

Through it all, my turtle pulsed in time to my heartbeat.

Nobody felt like sticking around after dinner, what with all the excitement beforehand. So we each took our leave of Riley and got our coats.

Tim came out to see us off. "I found an amazingly cheap flight to Mexico City," he said. "The drawback is that it leaves at six a.m."

"When will you be back?"

"I don't know," he said. "It depends on Ana's condition. Ernesto didn't know how bad it was."

I hugged him. "You take care of her, and bring her with you next time. I want to meet her."

He gave me a lopsided grin. "I will."

Gene hadn't yet returned. "Too embarrassed," I said to Riley.

She snorted. "Gene? Embarrassed? Are we talking about the same man?" Then she sobered. "I think he just needs some time alone to process what happened tonight. He did think he was getting away with it. He told me as much when we started seeing each other again." Then her lip curled. "I'm sure this is all a terrible blow to his ego."

"He's lucky he's not in jail," I said.

"He might be, before it's over," said Bea. "I have a duty as a physician to report certain things to the authorities, and child abuse is one of them."

"You'd turn in your own father?" Riley asked, shocked.

Bea looked uncomfortable. "I need to talk it over with John." She and her husband shared a look. "And with a lawyer. The statute of limitations has probably run out on most of his victims, but not the later ones. Of course, someone would have to come forward." She wrinkled her nose. "Or Dad would have to confess."

"I'll talk to him," Riley said. "He needs therapy, regardless. And I need to decide what *I'm* going to do next." She crossed her arms and looked around her, at the house she shared with Gene. "At least we don't have kids to worry about."

Ruth put a hand on her arm and squeezed. "You need to stick by him," she advised. "That's what a wife is supposed to do – cleave to her husband, no matter what."

Bea, Riley, and I exchanged glances. "Thanks, Ruth," Riley said, and uncrossed her arms to pat her on the shoulder. "I know."

Chapter 14

I got fired, of course. As soon as Dee heard that I wasn't going to be able to meet his deadline for coming back to work, he told me he was letting me go. "To be honest, I'd already hired somebody to fill your position," he said, when I called him that next morning. "I had a feeling you weren't going to be back."

"What if I *had* come back?" I said. "Would you have stuck me out on the floor as punishment for having a family emergency?"

"Hey, now," he said. "There's no call for that kind of talk."

I ignored him. "Because actually, that's against federal law. I looked it up. And it's also against the law to fire me for taking a leave of absence for a family member."

"You said she was your *ex*-mother-in-law," he said.

"So you're off the hook, then?" I said. "What if she hadn't been a relative at all, but someone who'd raised me?"

"The law's the law," he said stiffly. "You know, Maggie, you need to watch what you say to me. I could give you a reference so lousy that you'd never find another job in this town."

"I had no intention of asking you for a reference," I said.

That really ticked him off. "I'll have H.R. contact you about your final paperwork." *Click.*

I waited, but I didn't hear a door shut in my head — or anywhere else nearby. So the door I'd heard the night before must have been one that I shut myself. Because I had been clear then — and I was still clear — that I wasn't going to work for any more companies that didn't care for their employees.

I wasn't sure what that meant for my future work history. I was pretty sure most companies cared much more for money than they did for the people who helped them make their money. But maybe I'd land somewhere decent once I got back home.

I was reluctant to call Em again, but she needed to know the Big Family Secret. So I texted her, asking her to call me when she got a minute, and it was *not* about coming home to help with Nana.

Fifteen minutes later, my cell phone rang. "It's *really early here*, Mom," she said, sounding exasperated.

"You have a half-brother," I said without preamble, and then went through the whole explanation.

"Holy cats," she said. "That's a lot to take in. What did Dad do?"

"He threw a fit."

"No way!"

"Yes way," I said. "And then he took off. Riley says he probably needs time to process it. She says he thought nobody knew what was going on. He truly thought he was getting away with everything."

"But it turns out everybody knew."

"Right. And then he tried to pin the blame on me."

"Because clearly it was your fault that he boinked Aunt Debbie *years* before he met you," she scoffed. "Wow."

I nodded. "'Wow' pretty well sums it up."

"How's Nana doing?"

"Remarkably well," I said. "I think all the secrets were weighing her down. She was in a much better mood after she cried it all out – and especially after I told her Aunt Debbie might come home."

"I bet," she said. "Uh, Mom? Is Nana still planning to leave you the house?"

"That's a very good question," I said. "Why?"

"No special reason. I just thought that maybe now that you've outed her, she'd have thought better of her crazy idea."

"Maybe. The last I heard, she hadn't signed her new will yet. So there's still hope. Oh, Em? There's more news." And I told her about Tim, and about losing my job.

"Sorry to hear that, but you'll find something else," she said. "And I'm pretty sure Tim will be okay. If things don't work out with Ana for some reason, he can always go back to Europe."

"I guess," I said, "but I'm really hoping that he decides to stay home for a while."

"Define home," Em said.

"That's another very good question," I said.

I had to stop, then, and take Ruth to see Dr. Stein. He looked only mildly concerned about the incision that had troubled John. "It's red, but not as red as I'd expect if you had a bad infection. Does it hurt?" he asked her.

"No," she said.

"Ruth?" I said sternly.

She glared at me, but said, "Okay, all right. It twinges now and then. But that's all."

Dr. Stein looked at me. "I'm going to write her a prescription for an antibiotic."

"More pills," she groaned.

"But you only have to take these for two weeks," he said, turning to his laptop. "I don't think it's serious, but it's better to be safe than sorry." He hit a final key. "There. You can pick it up at the front window on your way out." He turned to Ruth. "Mrs. Brandt, everything looks good, so I won't need to see you again. It's been a pleasure." He held out his right hand and she shook it.

"Nice doing business with you, Doc," she said.

"My assistant is setting up your first radiation appointment for you," he said. "You can pick up that information on your way out, too." He turned to me then. "And it's been a pleasure to meet you, as well, Ms. Brandt." He took my hand and held it a little too long.

"Nice to meet you, too," I said with a smile, and withdrew my hand.

"You still have my card?"

"Yes, of course. I'll call if we need anything."

"Coffee," Ruth hissed.

"Coffee would be excellent," Dr. Stein said with a big smile. "Shall we say ten o'clock tomorrow morning? Unfortunately, we'll have to meet at the hospital cafeteria, as I'm booked there all day."

"Sure," I said. "That would be fine."

"Until tomorrow, then," he said, and preceded us out.

I held my tongue until we got outside. The temperature had dropped precipitously while we were inside, and a sharp breeze had sprung up. "You know," I said, gritting my teeth against the buffeting wind, "we had nearly gotten out of there without me having to agree to a date with him."

"I noticed," she said. She looked frail enough to take wing, but her tongue was still plenty sharp. "That's why I spoke up. *You* were going to let the opportunity pass you by."

"I'm not interested in him, Ruth!"

"How can you tell? You barely know him."

"I've seen his office," I said. "He's a neat freak. We'd never get along."

"He's got money. You could hire a maid."

I raised my hands in surrender. "Fine. If I get coffee with him and I still don't like him, will you leave it alone?"

She side-eyed me. "Maybe. I'll decide when I hear how the date went."

It was a disaster, of course. I was there in plenty of time. I got coffee and a Danish, and took a seat that was within full view of the door. No Nathan.

Half an hour went by. No Nathan.

By the time he showed up, I'd been waiting for nearly an hour. "I'm so very sorry," he said, scooting into the seat across from me. "The procedure I had this morning was supposed to be routine, but it took much, much longer than I expected." He sipped his coffee and grimaced. Then he said, "How are you with hearing about blood?"

"Not so good," I said, shaking my head.

"Oh." He seemed crestfallen. Then he perked up. "Well. What do you like to read?"

"I'm not much of a reader," I said. "Romance novels, occasionally, and the newspaper."

"Do you watch TV?"

"Hallmark Channel," I offered.

"What kinds of movies do you like?"

"Um…" I smiled brightly. "I saw 'Trainwreck' a couple of weeks ago. I thought Amy Schumer was hilarious."

"Do you ever watch any dramas?" He was starting to look desperate.

"Oh, no," I said, waving off the idea. "I would never. They're all too depressing."

"Ah. Well." He glanced at his watch. "I'm so sorry to cut this short, but I need to scrub up for my next procedure. And I apologize again that you had to wait so long."

"No problem," I said. "Nice talking to you."

He gulped the rest of his coffee, smiled, and ran for the door.

I couldn't help it – I burst out laughing. But not so loud that I didn't hear a door *snick* shut in my head.

Then I pulled out my phone and looked up show times for "The Danish Girl" – a drama, as it happened, that I very much wanted to see. Ruth was fully expecting coffee with Nathan to turn into lunch. I figured I had just enough time to squeeze in a matinee.

When I got back to Ruth's, I told her I had nothing in common with Dr. Stein, and anyway, he was no gentleman. Her face fell, but she tried to be philosophical about it. "At least you got out there. And you know what they say – you have to kiss a lot of frogs before you find a prince."

I laughed. "I haven't heard that one in at least ten years."

"Well, they *used* to say it," she muttered. "I wonder what's on TV."

I left her to her usual afternoon schedule and went upstairs to call Abby.

I didn't have to, as it turned out; both Debbie and Em had called her in the interim. But she was grateful to get an account of the big family meeting from someone who'd been there. "Did Gene ever show up again?" she asked.

I felt obscurely guilty. "I don't know. I haven't talked to Riley since the dinner."

"It's okay. I'll call. I should check on Gene anyway."

"Can I ask you something?"

She sounded wary. "Sure, I guess."

"How long did you know about it before you told your mother?"

She blew out a breath. "A while. They tried to get me in on their game, too, but I was really young – seven or eight. I thought boys were gross, and I had no interest at all in touching my brother's penis." She huffed a laugh. "Which makes sense, in retrospect."

"No kidding," I said. "What made you finally tell Ruth?"

"Oh, you'll enjoy this," she said. "I'd gone down to the basement to get something – I don't remember what, now, and it doesn't matter. Anyway, I heard this weird noise coming from behind the furnace, and it scared me to death, you know? So I ran upstairs and yelled for Ma. It turned out that they'd made themselves a little love nest back there, with all of our extra blankets and pillows."

I frowned. "Debbie told me you'd stumbled in on them in Gene's room when they forgot to lock the door."

"That was another time," she said. "And it wasn't Gene's room – it was ours. And they were doing it on *my* bed."

"Ew," I said.

"Exactly. Ma had gone to the store, and they thought I'd gone with her. I think that's when they moved to the basement."

"Wow." I shook my head. "What was it like to grow up with that?"

"It wasn't any fun," she said quietly. "Everybody blamed me. Gene and Debbie were mad at me for ratting them out, and Ma was mad at me for causing her to have to deal with it."

My eyes widened. "Do you think she knew what was going on?"

"Who knows, with her? Anyway, the only one who treated me like a human being was Daddy, and he was hardly ever home. And then Debbie had to go away to have the baby, and Ma made Gene move downstairs. Isolating him from the family was supposed to be his punishment. But he loved it because he could come and go as he pleased."

"And then Debbie never came back," I said.

"And Gene tried to mess around with me."

"Oh, no."

"Oh, yes. I had to punch him in the face to make him stop." She sighed. "At times I envied Deb. At least she didn't have to live with them anymore."

I shook my head. "I'm so sorry."

"Eh. It is what it is. I'm sure you had a crazy upbringing, too."

"Parts of it were tough," I said. *But none of it was anything like yours.*

As I ended the call with Abby, a horrible thought occurred to me. I immediately dialed Emmy. "Sorry to bug you again so soon," I said in a rush, "but I just have one question. Did your father ever…?"

"No."

"Never?"

"Never."

"Do you know if he…?"

"No, he never tried anything with Bea, either. You two must be on the same wavelength; I *just* got off the phone with her. Bea thinks he learned his lesson about fouling his own nest after he got Aunt Debbie pregnant."

Or after Abby punched him, maybe. "Okay. Thanks for setting my mind at ease."

"No problem, Mom. But please stop looking for trouble, okay? This thing is enough of a shitshow as it is."

"You're not wrong," I said.

Chapter 15

Debbie arrived, alone, about a week later. I was more than happy to let her have her old room back.

I skipped out on the mother-daughter reunion and went for a walk along Rock Creek instead. As I passed the entrance to the park, I noticed a Woodstock-vintage VW bus parked at the curb. I debated about knocking, and then shook my head and kept walking. What were the odds?

As I reached the signpost for the start of the trail, I heard the vehicle's side door slide back. "Hey!" a male voice called. "Maggie, isn't it?"

I turned and waved to Zed. Of course it was him. Who else would drive a scruffy van into my mother-in-law's neat neighborhood?

"Come on in and have some tea with us," he said. So I retraced my steps and hopped in.

"Hi, Granny," I said, taking her hands.

"You've had quite an adventure, I hear," she said. Today, she was dressed in a lilac tracksuit, and her white hair was piled in a messy bun atop her head. Zed, I'd noticed, was wearing exactly the same thing as when I'd met them at the Great Circle.

"Now how did you hear about my adventure?" I asked with a smile, as Zed handed around tea in battered mugs.

"Let's see her," she said, holding out her hand.

I didn't even pretend not to know what she was talking about; I just pulled off the turtle necklace and handed it over. She inspected it carefully, rubbing her thumb over the spots of bright copper where the tarnish had worn away. "Mm-hmm," she said, more than once.

"Is that good?" I asked finally, in a teasing tone.

"It's very good," she said, and handed it back. "You've done an excellent job with reclaiming this family. Of course, there's still more to do."

I thought of Abby, who hadn't quite yet forgiven her family for making her the scapegoat, and of Gene, who was still refusing Riley's insistence that he receive counseling. And of poor Riley herself, who had thought she'd caught a prize when Gene agreed to marry her. "Sure, but most of that will be their job," I said.

"And you've given them admirable tools to work with. Beatrice is an amazing young woman," Granny said. "She'll be instrumental in pulling them through the rough patches."

"She is pretty amazing," I said, trying not to puff up too much.

"Tim is healing nicely, too," she said. "That Mexican girl, Ana, is doing a good job with him. And Emily…"

"Emily was always fine," I said.

"She was the least affected," Granny corrected me. "But she's come through it well. There's just one more piece to this puzzle, but that will fall into place in time."

"You mean Lenny," I said. "Debbie's going to look for him."

"She won't find him. But rest assured, he'll turn up."

"That's good to hear." I finished my tea and handed the mug back to Zed. "I should go. Thanks for checking in on me."

"Of course," Zed said. "It's what we do."

I gave Granny a hug as Zed slid open the side door. As I passed him, I said, "Will I see you again?"

"Of course," he said again. Then he grinned. "We're always right around the corner."

As I headed back to the trail, Granny called from the open door, "You did the right thing with that Dr. Stein, running him off the way you did. He's someone else's project."

"I knew it from the get-go," I said. "Goodbye, Granny."

"Bye, Margie!"

"It's Maggie," I heard Zed say.

"Bye, Maggie!"

I laughed and waved as I turned toward the park.

The next night, we gathered at Bea's for a farewell dinner. Royce was anxious to show me all her toys, and Ryker claimed me as his personal jungle gym when he wasn't crawling all over Ruth. I was sorry to be going home, if only because of those two.

Debbie was taking over my duties as her mother's nursemaid for the next couple of weeks. "I'm just sorry I couldn't get here soon enough to save your job," she said. Her Southern drawl was rapidly disappearing, now that she was back in Maryland.

"It's okay," I said. "Really. I don't think I was ever meant to stay there very long."

Gene and Riley arrived late and left early. They put on a good show, but it was clear they weren't getting along. Gene hugged his sister once, and then stayed so far away from her that she might as well have been radioactive. Which, in his case, might have been the truth. I mulled over whether he preferred young girls because he couldn't have his sister. I'd have to ask Bea what she thought of that theory later.

All too soon, the evening was over. And all too early the next morning, I hit the road for Indiana.

The weather was outstanding for mid-November in the Midwest: crisp but dry. I made good time across Pennsylvania and the first part of Ohio. I debated whether to stop at the Great Circle again, but I had the sense that I'd already learned as much about the past as I needed to know for right now. And I also had a feeling that I needed to keep driving – that there was an appointment I needed to keep, or someone I needed to meet.

At last, I pulled off I-75 north of Cincinnati to gas up. I made a wrong turn going into the truck stop and ended up parking with the eighteen-wheelers.

As I got out of the car, I saw a familiar form ahead of me, walking to the restrooms. He wore a leather jacket, jeans, and cowboy boots – clothing Gene would never have worn in his life – but his posture and his stride were an exact match to my ex-husband's.

I hurried to catch up to him. "Leonard?" I called, realizing that I could be wasting my time. It might not be him, for one thing; and even if it was him, his adoptive parents might have renamed him.

But no, he turned and stopped. "Ma'am?" he said, in Gene's voice but with a Louisiana drawl.

I was breathless when I reached him. "This is going to seem like an odd question," I said, "but by any chance, are you adopted?"

"Lady," he said with a broad grin that looked just like Debbie's, "you have just made my day!"

I learned over coffee that Lee Hastings (he'd never gone by Lenny) had been adopted by a couple from Baton Rouge. His adoptive parents had always been candid with him that he was not their biological child. "They're wonderful people," he said. "I couldn't ask for better. But still, you always wonder."

"Sure," I said. "That's only natural."

He had sought information about his birth family from the adoption agency many years before, but he'd hit the same brick wall Debbie had: closed adoption, no information available. It was just recently that he'd begun thinking about trying again. "In fact, just this morning, I made myself a vow that I would not take no for an answer this time. And then here I run into you, Ms. Brandt," he said, with an engaging grin so like his mother's that I had to grin back. "It's like God was looking out for me today."

"I expect He was," I said.

I gave him Debbie's contact information, and mine. And then I hit the road again, my turtle gently warming the spot above my heart.

It's not a long drive from Cincinnati to Lawrenceburg, Indiana. But it was long enough for me to come down from the high of stumbling across Lee/Leonard/Lenny and begin to contemplate my own mess. I had an apartment to go back to, but no way to keep paying the rent without a job. I could move back in with my mother, but I needed to talk to her about it – and I had been so busy with solving the mysteries in Ruth's family that I hadn't spoken to her in a couple of weeks. I had told myself, in odd moments, that no news was good news – that if something bad had happened, either my cousin Sandy or his wife would have called me.

But that rationalization wasn't cutting it any more. So after a good night's rest in my own bed, I drove over to Mom's house – my childhood home. I parked on the concrete pad in front of the garage and let myself in at the chain-link gate.

As I walked up the sidewalk to the porch, Mom opened the door and stared at me through the window in the storm door. I smiled and reached for the knob – and quick as lightning, she clicked the lock on the storm door into place.

"Mom?" I said, confused.

"You need to leave," she warned me.

"Mom, it's me. Maggie. Your daughter."

"I don't have a daughter named Maggie," she insisted, glaring. "Now beat it, or I'll call the cops."

There was that gut punch again. *When had Mom's mind gone? Why hadn't Sandy and Diane called me?* I fell back a step, preparing to get in my car and drive to Indianapolis to have it out with my brother and his wife. But just as I began to turn on my heel, I felt a warm pulse upon my chest. I pulled my necklace out from under my shirt. "See this?" I said, brandishing it at my mother.

"Oh! That's Margie's!" she said, her face wreathed suddenly in smiles. She flipped the lock up and opened the door wide for me. "Come on in, and I'll tell you how she came to have it."

I smiled weakly and went inside, still clutching the effigy. It seemed my next challenge had already been picked out for me.

As if in confirmation, my turtle buzzed in my hand.

Author's Note

In August 2016, I stumbled across the Great Circle Earthworks in Newark, Ohio, in much the same way Maggie does here, although I had to see the sign on I-70 twice before I decided to pull off the highway and figure out what it meant. Over the years, the Great Circle has been used as a Civil-War-era military training ground, a horse-racing park, an amusement park, and a county fairgrounds. But somehow the berms and ditch have survived, and there's still a sense, as you stand within the circle, that the place is sacred.

The Newark Earthworks, of which the Great Circle is a part, has been shortlisted for designation as a UNESCO World Heritage Site. As backup for the nomination, a group of scholars contributed essays about the Newark site to *The Newark Earthworks: Enduring Monuments, Contested Meanings*, edited by Lindsay Jones and Richard D. Shiels. I recommend the book to anyone interested in learning more about the site.

The Hopewell weren't the only mound builders. Sci-fi author Robert Silverberg wrote a non-fiction book about these cultures in the late 1960s; I picked up the abridged version, called *The Mound Builders*, and found it to be eminently readable. Nothing is known about these ancient cultures apart from the archaeological record, and Silverberg does a great job of highlighting how white men's prejudices shaped what they believed about the mounds and their builders, and how those fears changed over time. It's almost as interesting a story as that of the mounds themselves.

Speaking of fear: Embarking on a new series is always a little daunting, but I'm looking forward to writing more of Maggie's adventures over the course of two more books.

Big thanks go once again to my editors, Susan Strayer and Kat Milyko. Suzu went above and beyond the call this time by driving me to Mound City, another Hopewell site in Ohio, as well as Shrum Mound, an Adena Culture site in Columbus. (I might have gone a little Indian-mound crazy while researching this book. I still need to plan my own trip to Cahokia…)

Thanks, too, to beta readers Melissa Bowersock and Laurie Boris, each of whom are awesome authors in their own right. Go read their work, if you haven't already.

If you enjoyed this book – or not – I'd love it if you would go back where you purchased it and post a review. Reviews are a key way that readers find good books, and I treasure each and every review that my books receive.

You're also warmly invited to join my Woo-Woo Team. We meet on Facebook at https://www.facebook.com/groups/WooWooTeam/. You have to ask to join, but so far I've let everybody in, so your odds of acceptance are spectacular. I'd love to see you there.

One more thing: To get the first word on all of my new releases, go to http://eepurl.com/xxw9d to sign up for my spam-free newsletter. It's your guaranteed way to find out what's coming up, and I only darken your inbox with them three or four times a year.

Lynne Cantwell
March 2017

About the Author

Lynne Cantwell writes mostly urban fantasy and paranormal romance, with a dash of magic realism when she's feeling more serious. She is also a contributing author for Indies Unlimited. In a previous life, she was a broadcast journalist who worked at Mutual/NBC Radio News, CNN, and a bunch of other places you have probably never heard of. She has a master's degree in fiction writing from Johns Hopkins University. Currently, she lives near Washington, D.C.

Discover other titles by Lynne Cantwell:

The Pipe Woman Chronicles Universe
Seized: Book One of the Pipe Woman Chronicles
Fissured: Book Two of the Pipe Woman Chronicles
Tapped: Book Three of the Pipe Woman Chronicles
Gravid: Book Four of the Pipe Woman Chronicles
Annealed: Book Five of the Pipe Woman Chronicles
The Pipe Woman Chronicles Omnibus

Where Were You When: A Land, Sea, Sky Anthology
Crosswind: Land, Sea, Sky Book 1
Undertow: Land, Sea, Sky Book 2
Scorched Earth: Land, Sea, Sky Book 3
The Land Sea Sky Trilogy

Dragon's Web: Book One of the Pipe Woman's Legacy

Firebird's Snare: Book Two of the Pipe Woman's Legacy
Spider's Lifeline: Book Three of the Pipe Woman's Legacy
Turtle's Weir: Book Four of the Pipe Woman's Legacy

A Billion Gods and Goddesses: The Mythology Behind *The Pipe Woman Chronicles*

Stand-Alone Novels
SwanSong
The Maidens' War
Seasons of the Fool

Short Story Collections
Back Home Again: The Five59 Stories, plus a few

Contributor
Indies Unlimited 2012 Flash Fiction Anthology
Indies Unlimited 2013 Flash Fiction Anthology
Indies Unlimited 2014 Flash Fiction Anthology
Indies Unlimited Tutorials and Tools for Prospering in a Digital World
Indies Unlimited Tutorials and Tools for Prospering in a Digital World, Vol. II
13 Bites
Summer Dreams
Boo!: Volume 2
Winter Tales
Plan 559 from Outer Space
Other Realms
13 Bites Vol. III
I Heard It on the Radio
Plan 559 from Outer Space Mk. II

Other Realms Volume II
13 Bites Vol. IV

Find Lynne on Teh Intarwebz:

Facebook: http://www.facebook.com/pages/Lynne-Cantwell
Twitter: http://twitter.com/lynnecantwell
Google Plus: http://plus.google.com/+LynneCantwell
Goodreads:
http://www.goodreads.com/author/show/696603.Lynne_Cantwell
Blog: http://www.hearth-myth.com

www.ingramcontent.com/pod-product-compliance
Lightning Source LLC
Chambersburg PA
CBHW050736230626
47052CB00002BA/384